To Theresa
Best Wishes

John Lennon

29/4/'16

HOME

HOME

JOHN DUNNE

Purtock Press
Portlaoise

First published in 2016 by
Purtock Press
13 Woodlawn
Portlaoise
County Laois
R32 A27H
Ireland
www.portlaoisepictures.com

ISBN: 978-1-5262-0210-9

Nearly all the characters in Part I of this book are fictional and any resemblence to anyone living or dead is mostly coincidental.

The quotation on page 112 is from *The Lonesome Death of Hattie Carroll* by Bob Dylan. Copyright © 1964, 1966 by Warner Bros. Inc.; renewed 1992 by Special Rider Music. All rights reserved. International copyright secured. Reprinted by permission.

Cover image © John Dunne Jnr.
Printed by PRINTcentral, Portlaoise

For

Denise, Neil, Gary, Aoife, John, and Tom

CONTENTS

I

II

I

THE KING AND QUEEN OF FOLK

She made her mind up for once and for all. No more nights tearing through sleepy midland towns. No more being groped in the back of the van, or crushed against the wall of windswept parish halls. No more feeling foolish in those stupid costumes, a monogrammed guitar hiding her breasts from the eyes of drooling bogmen. And what had she to show for five years of playing relief, five years imagining her name in lights over Roseland, Cloudland, Dreamland? A fake wedding ring she hadn't worn since 1954, a guitar she couldn't play, two Annie Oakley outfits she hated but, for some obscure reason, couldn't leave behind, £5. 10s. hidden in the lining of her boot. God knows why she picked this town but, within days, she had a job in a chip shop and a flat near the statue in the Square.

Φ

Three weeks before the Leaving Cert, he crept into his granny's room and stole fistfuls of her savings. The same morning, he left a note on the hallstand – 'It's alright, Ma, I'm only sightseeing' – and thumbed a lift to Dublin. A fortnight later, a postcard of the Golden Gate Bridge trembled in his mother's hand. 'Don't be worrying, Ma, I'm living in a grand place. Love and peace to granny and yourself.' Throughout the Summer of Love, that postcard withered on the mantelpiece, the dried tear a hazy UFO over San Francisco Bay.

Haight-Ashbury was all his album covers suddenly come to life. He slept on the floor of a rainbow-coloured warehouse, pressed between bodies that exuded incense and gyrated naked through his dreams. In Golden Gate Park he met a girl from Oregon who painted tulips on his face and frightened him by wanting to make love in the middle of the crowd. They hitched to Monterey and, for weeks afterwards, Pete Townshend windmilled past his eyes, Hendrix's guitar exploded in his brain. He busked to queues outside the Fillmore, bawling psychedelic versions of *The Sea Around Us*, *Boolavogue*, *McAlpine's Fusiliers*. In a doorway on Pine Street, he drank from a barrel of spiked orange juice and ran in screaming circles, pursued by fiery ten pound notes.

He survived the Summer of Love by begging and on food provided by the Diggers. In mid-August, flat broke and homesick, he robbed a Chinese laundry and fled in terror to the airport. The morning his classmates awaited their results, he swaggered from the station in a paisley shirt and love beads, terrified of what his mother was going to say.

Φ

"Have ya e'er a breast?"

"Howaya fixed for after? Are ya hittin' Danceland?"

She soon learned to ignore the sniggers, the drunken offers to wait for her outside. All she had to do was think of something else. Sometimes she stared at the photograph of Padre Pio until his hands dripped ketchup on the counter. Sometimes she remembered a story Sister Agnes used to tell them. She could see the soldiers dangling the little girl over a vat of boiling oil; their teeth stripped like dogs, barking that she had never seen a vision, never spoken to a lady in the grotto. She saw the oil spitting at the girl's feet, her mouth screaming for Our Lady. She wondered what it must be like to have a family of your own. What would you do if your own little one had to suffer like that? What would you do if someone you loved was squashed beneath a lorry or, like Sister Majella, gone to skin and bone from cancer?

"Give us a single and a burger out of trap four."

Φ

Every time he passed the bank, the same idea flitted through his mind; the guitars, the records, the clothes he could buy. No guilt at all; just the simple fear of being caught. He killed the days in Alo Donegan's, trying out different guitars, sneering at records by the Royal Showband, the Miami, anyone who wasn't groovy. When Alo told him to get lost, he stood peering through the window, his hair a crow's nest that scandalised old women on the footpath. He bored his friends with how music liberates your mind; why none of the English crowd could hold a candle to Dylan, Jefferson Airplane, Country Joe and the Fish.

At home every conversation turned into a row.

"Would you not go back and try again? You always had the brains to burn."

"I told you, Ma, I'm not interested. You think I'm doing nothing, but I am. I'm getting my head together for the music. I'm going to start a group."

His grandmother reached for her stick. "You ought to be ashamed of yourself, so you should. Your poor mother left on her own and you out gallivanting. Look at the cut of you. I never thought I'd see the day a grandson of mine would turn out to be a woman."

"Shush, Mammy, you're only upsetting yourself."

"What are you shushing me for? Isn't it the truth? As true as I'm sitting here, that's what he is. A woman. Look at the head of him. And you're worse to stand for it. And look

3

what he did to me. If Paddy was alive, he'd take him by the scruff of the neck and land him back in school.'

"Leave my father out of this!"

Φ

Images from Holy Angels appeared before her in the darkness. She left the light on, but the minute she closed her eyes, they came again. Fingers bleeding in the sewing room. The morning she awoke with blood on her thighs. The darkness shaking with the voice of Holy God. There is no room in Heaven for bold girls, dirty girls who destroy their nice clean sheets. She saw Sister Majella in Annie Oakley's buckskin, the guitar poised above her like an axe. She jerked awake and fell forward, sobbing on the bedclothes. When her lips stopped trembling, she parted the curtains and gazed across the Market Square. *O clement, O loving, O sweet Virgin Mary, please take away the pain.*

Φ

To finally get rid of him, Alo let him have the guitar for £2 down and five shillings a week. He swaggered home, sanded down the sunburst finish and painted the body seven different colours. Along the psychedelic whorls he printed THIS MACHINE KILLS SHOWBANDS

"Where are you going with that yoke? Would you not take up a real instrument? The tin whistle or the melodeon?"

"The guitar is the voice of revolution."

"What?"

"Freedom flows from the strings of the guitar."

"Will you whisht! If your Daddy could hear this Baluba music he'd turn in his grave."

Φ

4

Now and then, out of the blue, she heard the tuning-fork. A needlepoint of sound that flashed from Sister Majella's fingers and pierced the scent of beeswax. For one hour a week, she wasn't a young woman in a child's pinafore, a skivvy feeding cabbage soup to rows of snivelling girls. Her voice found the note and followed Sister Majella's hands. *Tantum ergo sacramentum, venermur cernui.* She loved the mystery of the words, how her own mouth, the lips that seldom moved except to answer questions, could shape the sound and direct it towards the stained-glass windows. The happiest day of her life was when Sister Majella died and she was chosen to sing at her funeral. She closed her eyes and felt the words rise from deep inside her; saw them soar above the bowed heads, the coffin with its four black candles, and vanish into clouds of incense. When Father Nugent smiled, her heart leapt like the infant in Saint Elizabeth's womb.

Φ

A girl in a KISS ME QUICK hat opened the door.

"Howaya."

"Tune in, turn on, drop out."

The room was crammed. Bodies slumped against the walls, bodies clinging to each other as *A Whiter Shade of Pale* coiled through the smoke. A boy with a Beatle haircut staggered towards him.

"Good man Hippie, we thought you weren't coming. What's that in your hair?"

"Where's Jimmy?"

"Passed out ages ago. We're on the beer all day."

When the music stopped, the boy bawled into the crowd: "D'ye want a sing-song? Hippie has the machine."

A space was cleared and a bottle of something thrust into his hand. He took a swig and started *Visions of Johanna.*

After the first verse, the hum of conversation rose; during the second, *The Hucklebuck* erupted from the speakers. He cursed into the noise, and was turning towards the door when the girl approached him.

"So you're the famous Hippie?"

The English accent surprised him.

"And you're not from the town."

"I'm here on holiday."

He felt the warm waft of vodka and wondered how drunk she was.

"How did you get in with this crowd?"

"James brought me, but he seems more interested in his mates."

"Do you want to sit down?"

He was spellbound by the stories of her life in London. The Marquee, the Roundhouse, Dylan in the Albert Hall...

"You really should come over. James says you're only wasting your time here."

Feet suddenly whirled by them and scattered the contents of her handbag.

"Here, I'll do it. You could be trampled to death in here. Do you feel like a breath of fresh air?"

"Don't mind if I do."

"There's a garden out the back."

She smiled with her eyes and followed him outside.

"At least it's safer than inside."

"Is it?" she smiled again and squeezed his hand.

Carefully, he stood his guitar against the wall and drew her towards him. He stared into her closed eyes and, as her tongue touched his, he eased her handbag open and slipped the purse into the back pocket of his jeans.

Φ

She never said to herself: why am I still here? I am not a

child; why am I answering doors, scrubbing floors, washing dirt from someone else's clothes? She never said a word; just walked from the chapel and out the wicket gate. It was so easy it frightened her. Only when her legs began to ache did she stop to look behind. The city was a mantilla of light in the distance, the sky the black cloth over Sister Majella's coffin. All that night she cowered in a shed that reeked of animals. When the sky turned grey, she snatched a dress from a clothesline and ran until her throat burned. That afternoon, a lorry stopped beside her and she blurted out the name of somewhere she had seen on a signpost. The driver looked her up and down and told her to get in. When she wouldn't answer any more of his questions, he handed her a sandwich, lit a cigarette and squinted at her breasts.

The moon above the service station was Jesus held aloft on Father Nugent's fingers. She heard music from somewhere down the road and, when the driver came back from the toilet, she was gone.

Edging through the parked cars, she wondered how a tent could be so big. A huge canvas room, longer than the refectory, full of music and feet hammering a wooden floor.

"Howaya Gorgeous."

She turned and found herself faced by a man old enough to be her father.

"Are you fond of the music?"

She heard herself telling him about the choir at home; how music always made her happy, even when she couldn't understand the words. No, she wasn't from the village, she was on holidays from Dublin. A story from the Bible ran through her head and she told him how she had got separated from her friends; how they, thinking she must have gone on ahead, were probably at home by now.

In all her life she had never said so much to anyone at once. And he believed every word. She knew by the way he smiled; by the way he nodded when she told him that her good clothes were in the car. She knew he believed her because he offered her a place to stay. She knew he was nice because he put a finger to her lips and told her not to wake Mammy. She threw her arms around his neck and begged him to look after her. She fell to her knees and pawed him like a dog. He lifted her up and undid the buttons of her dress. Next evening, she followed him aboard the ferry that would bring him back to building sites and half a room in Kilburn. As she caressed his face and gazed across the water, her new life rose before her like a beam of light, a shining path leading Holy Mary into heaven.

Φ

"He's a bit of a bollocks alright."

"It's the poor mother I feel sorry for."

"Someone said he's taking drugs as well."

The shirts, the hair, the sunglasses, became a legend in the town. A legend soon twisted into notoriety. When a row broke out in the Macra, two bouncers dragged him from his chair and bundled him outside. When a bikini appeared on the Blessed Virgin, Mr. Clear told Father Ging how he remembered him in the shop, inspecting tins of paint.

The truth was that he was guilty of none of this. He had, he patiently explained to his mother, one fundamental ideological difference with the Hippie Movement. No drugs. No way José. Absolutely no drugs. The Age of Aquarius must not be defiled by chemicals. The future would not come from altered states of mind. The revolution must be forged from the strings of a guitar.

"I worry about your state of mind, so I do. Locked up in that room, not knowing whether it's day or night."

"I'm writing songs."

"You're what?" His grandmother craned forward in

her chair.

"Writing my own songs."

"Begob, that beats Banagher. A composer. And you wouldn't do your Leaving."

Φ

The first time he beat her, she threw the ring across the floor and walked the streets until his headlights impaled her to a wall. The second time, she screamed and warned him never to lay a finger on her again. The third time, she fell into his arms, begging his forgiveness, swearing to do anything he wanted if he wouldn't leave her on her own. When it happened again, she hung around the Galtymore until the band had finished and she found the courage to ask if they would like to hear her sing. The following Friday night they asked to hear her again, and so began ten years of traipsing around the pubs and halls of North London until, in 1962, she walked on to a stage in Ireland, a grinning cowgirl with a monogrammed guitar.

Φ

He practised until his fingers bled. When they could take no more, he fell back on the bed, closed his eyes and walked on to the stage at Newport. He chopped and changed everything he learned until he had chords and melodies of his own. Pacing the room, fists clenched, he prayed for words to fit the tunes. He stared into the mirror and, in his bloodshot eyes, saw the voice of his generation suffering for his art.

One night he found his mother slumped in her armchair. He stood for a moment, startled by the shiver of tenderness, the surge of love unlike anything he'd ever felt before. Is this what it all comes to, he asked himself, twenty years of working your fingers to the bone? As her breathing filled the kitchen, he remembered her tears the morning he came back from San Francisco, her arms around him on the doorstep, pleading with him never to break her heart again.

With a small cry she awoke and rubbed her eyes.

"I got a fright. I thought there was someone standing over me."

"You were only dreaming. Would you like a cup of cocoa?"

"No thanks, pet. What time is it?"

"Late. You should be in bed."

"I'll go up in a minute." She sighed and looked away from him. "What are you going to do?"

"I'll just make a cup of tea and go back up."

"I meant... what are you going to do... your future."

"Please Ma, don't start again. I'm a musician. A song-writer."

"Will you stop! How do you think I feel? My only child locked up in a room like a lunatic... talking to himself."

"I'm getting my head together. Music is the–"

"Music! A lot of happiness music ever brought into this house. I always prayed that you would be different. Your father broke my heart and now you're doing it too."

"If he hadn't been so fond–"

"Don't speak like that about your Daddy. We gave you everything you ever wanted, and look at the thanks we got. You broke my heart by running away like that, and now you won't go back to school... or do a hand's turn around the house. Do you think I'm made of stone?"

"Please Ma, stop crying, you'll only wake granny."

"You broke my heart so you did. My own flesh and blood, all I have left in the world, and you went and broke my heart."

Φ

She ignored them all. The men in suits who looked funny

asking for more vinegar. Young lads smirking through a daze of beer. Voices lurking in doorways. Voices flung from cars as she walked home alone. Letters from London, promising the earth.

Φ

He never told her how he'd found out she was a singer. He just strolled in one evening and asked her if she wanted to be famous.

"What?"

"You and me. The King and Queen of Folk."

"You must be joking."

"I'm serious. I have the songs, you have the looks."

"Stop coddin'. Do you want salt and vinegar?"

Φ

"This is a lovely one... *Tantum ergo sacramentum...*"

"Did you ever hear tell of the singing nun?"

"Who?"

"It doesn't matter. Listen. Here's the new one I'm working on:

Let's make it in the field, let's make it in the park,
Let's make it in the daylight, let's make it in the dark".

"What do you think?"

"What are you making?"

Φ

Happiness took her by surprise. She squeezed his hand and told him how music wiped away the past. He was amazed by how she sang his words as if she believed every single one. When she said she was tired, he lulled her into sleep

11

with lies about America. When he went on and on about the voice of revolution, she wondered what she was letting herself in for. When he burst in one night and said they had bookings in November, she said no, she couldn't face it. Next morning she handed in her notice.

Φ

"But what's the smell?"
"What smell?
"It's like... dogs."
"He used to bring greyhounds to the track in Kilkenny. It'll wear off. Will you give us a hand, or are you going to stand there giving out?"
"Where can I hang my suit?"
"What?"
"My suit. Where can I hang it? Look, it's creased already."
"Jesus, didn't I tell you not to bring that yoke."
"But what am I going to wear?"
"I don't care what you wear, but I'm not going on stage with Buffalo fucking Bill."
"But I have to dress up."
"Listen, it's either me or that outfit."

Φ

And so the first hippie in the Midlands and his ageing beehive blonde set out for their first engagement in a pub in Tullamore. As the van bounced along the bog road, she asked him to slow down. In reply, he opened the window and his hair streaming in the wind made him feel like a musician. Outside Killeigh she asked him again. She was thinking of Sister Majella lying in her coffin when suddenly he swore. The last thing she saw was a little girl talking to

Our Lady.

Φ

Most of us can remember the year, some can name the month or season, others can pin it down to a particular day or night, but he could remember the precise moment he fell in love. 7.15 pm, Friday, November 10, 1967. His first thought was: this is how my mother felt the morning I came home from San Francisco. *Someone who will die for you and more.* Every time she brushed my hair, kissed away a headache, cried on my First Communion picture. At exactly 7.15 on that wet November evening, as somewhere down the corridor a radio played *Massachusetts*, he stared at the bed and saw a small animal squealing in a trap, his father weeping on his deathbed.

It had nothing to do with sex. He had never seen her naked, never touched her, never even wanted to. Was it the tear that did it? The thread of blood on her chin? The memory of her face when they pulled her from the van? Was it the way her eyes wouldn't open when he screamed her name?

The single tear hung like a glass bead from the corner of her eye. As he took a tissue to wipe her cheek, his hand froze in mid-air. For the rest of his life he wondered if he'd been hallucinating, if the drugs on Pine Street were still lurking in his brain. He saw her kneel before him, the stitches in her face twitch like insects as she begged him not to leave her. In the days that followed, he never worried about how little they had in common or what the town was sure to say. He never looked at her and thought: she's nearly old enough to be my mother.

Φ

In a basement in Rathmines, he hit a chord and waited for it to die away. He played the chord a second time, listened

13

intently, and told the landlord he'd move in on Sunday evening.

His mother wanted to know if he was stone mad. He said no, I'm in love. She warned him never to darken her door again. He threw the note on to the hallstand – 'Don't criticise what you don't understand' – and slammed the door behind him.

In her room, he found her on her knees, gazing at the statue, her face caked with powder, her neck so white he saw how easy it would be to cut someone's throat.

"I have everything packed."

"I'm not carrying those yokes to the station."

When she started to cry, he kissed her scars and draped the suits across his arm.

Φ

For the first few months he could understand her silence, how she sat for hours, the mirror trembling in her hand. He kept telling her about a girl he knew in San Francisco:

"Honest to God. Savaged by a pack of bears and, one morning, the scars disappeared. Just like that."

He swore her face made no difference:

"Look, sure I'm no oil-painting myself. Wait, I nearly forgot. I bought you a present… What do you think?"

"Is it a box? A jewellery box?"

"It's a hat… a leopardskin pillbox hat… really the expensive kind… here, try it on…"

The walls were closing in and he grew to hate those tears, the way her mouth quivered an apathetic 'no'.

Φ

Normally he resented her prayer-meetings, but tonight he didn't care if she never came home. No mirror, no tears, no wanting to tell her to shut the fuck up. He could tidy the place, switch off the lights, close his eyes and wait for *Blonde on Blonde* to galvanise the dark. Where did she put that incense..? He cursed her, he cursed himself, he cursed his mother; he cursed the owner of the van. She'd be back any minute and the night, his night, would be ruined. He eventually found her note sticking from the sleeve of *John Wesley Harding*. 'I'm going away for good and I'm bringing the suits. God bless.'

WINGS

Martin Lalor never knew his mother. She died bringing him to life and was hardly cold in the ground when his father demanded the infant from the nurses. A week later, he left the Council's new estate and returned to live with his mother and her invalid sister. The family home was a tradesman's cottage lurking in a lane off Grattan Street.

Growing up, Martin was known to schoolfriends as the quiet lad who 'lived with the two oul' ones'; to his teachers he was always the bright, courteous pupil who showed little or no interest in his work. But every evening after supper, the spelling and arithmetic were pushed away and Martin Lalor became a completely different child. From her bed, Aunt Mary mesmerised him with the heroic ancient sagas, the tragic history of Ireland. Plundering the centuries, the hoarse masculine mouth spat a litany of outrage and glorious revenge. Leaning forward, breathless with emotion, she shook rosary beads at Martin and cursed every Laois-man who ever joined the RIC. Her face was prayerful as she named the brave young local lads who burned out Harcourt House; her black eyes danced as she recalled the one survivor squealing like a *banbh* across the fiery midnight lawn.

Φ

In the early summer of 1974, a week before his son's fifteenth birthday, John Lalor travelled by train to Dublin. Throughout the journey, dreading his appointment with the specialist, he stared at his fingernails or through the window at the undulating wires. He worried about the tightness in his throat, his alarming loss of weight, but most of all he feared what might become of Martin.

That afternoon, beaming in the knowledge that the growth could be removed, he emerged into the sunshine and found himself with hours to kill before his train. He took a bus to the city centre and, suddenly remembering his mother reading out the advertisement for the half-price sale in Guineys, walked straight into the bomb in Talbot Street.

Φ

Over the next few years, Martin was usually dismissed as either harmless or odd. While his schoolmates followed convent girls or marvelled at the airport noises on *The Dark Side of the Moon*, he was always seen alone. Occasionally he would break his silence and stop reluctant acquaintances – sometimes even total strangers – with incoherent mono-logues on the boyhood of Cuchulain, Mad Sweeney's flight through Ireland, Cromwell's devastation of the Rock of Dunamaise.

Φ

Towards midnight on December 31, 1978, the faithful of this drowsy Midland town converged upon the statue in the Square. Poised behind the microphone in a furry Russian hat, the young priest cleared his throat and invited them to sing a hymn to Mary. On their knees, reminding themselves of the figures in the manger, they sought her intercession throughout the coming year.

Behind the war memorial, Martin Lalor stood and strained to hear the murmur of their prayers. Suddenly, he shook the sweat from his hair, wiped his eyes, and stepped back again to swing his father's sledgehammer. In steady rhythmic arcs, he attacked the stone then, resting for a moment, like a blindman touching someone's face, traced the pulverised inscription with his fingers.

He was sobbing at the treachery of the Leinsters when the car pulled up behind him. Turning quickly, he brandished the hammer at the hesitating Guards.

"The *Gae Bolga*! Beware the *Gae Bolga*!"

"C'mon now Martin, the Granny's wondering where you are. C'mon like a good lad, give us that yoke now."

In reply, the hammer hurtled through the air, above the crackling voices in the car, and slid along the frosty ground.

Φ

One irate Councillor demanded that the delinquent be charged with defacing public property. Kids in discos marvelled at how he thought he was Cuchulain. A local doctor gave a lecture to the Golf Club on the signs of hebephrenia. The sisters' favourite priest pestered them with parables on the waywardness of youth. What eventually happened was this: the town decided it had enough of Martin Lalor and so, one January morning, he found himself ascending the steps of St. Fintan's, Father Ging beside him, cheerfully repeating that it was only for a day or two, a week at the outside, just for a little rest.

That first afternoon, he bemused the nurses with his adventures in the wonderland of Irish myth. His eyes leered with pleasure when his arms were Aoife's legs clenched around his back. With tears streaming down his neck, he hacked at his beloved Ferdia. Cowering in a corner of the room, he shuddered at the Morrigan's curse of heifer, wolf and eel...

Φ

As aimlessly as cattle in a meadow, the patients shuffled around the ward. Martin peered at them through the glass panel, then nonchalantly walked along the corridor, pausing now and then to sniff at cabbage, piss and futile disinfectant. He passed the porter's vacant desk, pulled his jacket tight around him, and strode along the avenue to the road. Past the church railings and the still, congested river; up the hill, past the barracks and the football field, out into the darkness of the countryside.

Φ

"That's it so for another day. Are you sure you'll be alright?"

"Of course I shall. I just need some assistance with the stairs."

"Well, I'll be off then, Miss. I'll be in again first thing in the morning."

"Thank you, Nan, and goodnight to you."

While Iris Harcourt sat before the bedroom mirror, Martin Lalor struggled with an outhouse door. Fingering wisps of hair, she sighed and reached for her comb. Cursing the darkness, he groped until he found a crowbar. As the withered fingers fumbled with her buttons, he padded through the kitchen. While she sat for a moment, irritated by the ladder in her stocking, he stood on the landing, his eyes fixed on the sliver of light beneath her door. She was wondering if Nan had turned the cooker off when the handle turned and his screech convulsed her tidy room.

Φ

Faster than the hound, Caoilte sped along the forest floor. Crashing through branches, the curse of Ronan thundering in his head, Sweeney traversed the wintry trees of Ireland. His face a weeping mask of pain, Martin Lalor stumbled through the depths of Togher Wood. On and on until, finally, on his hands and knees, senseless with exhaustion, clutching at tufts of grass, he tumbled over a low ditch. For an instant he lay on the icy ground, then picked himself up and, flapping outstretched arms, ran, fell, and ran again until he reached the bridge.

Φ

In the townland of Togher, like the woman who met the *púca* in her garden, or the man who still used horses in the fields, Radar Coughlan was regarded with benevolent suspicion. He could detect, so the stories went, whose dog provoked the howling midnight uproar; what caused the nocturnal rustling in the hedge, even, he once proclaimed, the height, sex, and destination of anyone passing his cottage in the dark. But tonight, leaning on his saddle at the foot of Railway Hill, Radar was baffled. He lowered his bicycle, un-hooked the flashlamp, and cautiously approached the bridge. Halfway up the slope, he craned his neck to listen.

Amused that he had come upon some drunken neighbour, he drew a long breath and resumed his pace. As soon as the light appeared, Martin Lalor sprang to life and leapt up on the parapet. Silhouetted against the moonlight, reeling with the frenzy of flight, he flailed at the incandescent stars, and for one miraculous moment, seemed to hover.

EEL

My father always claimed that it was his greyhound who saw them first. He was walking her along the Green Road when – and I quote – all of a sudden she started leppin' and bawlin' like a feckin' eejit. Others maintained that it was Mrs. Lalor going to Mass, or Seanie Doran coming from the night shift at the mill. Who knows? but by eight o'clock the town was hopping. Where did they come from? Did they wriggle up out of drains, fall off a lorry, get lost looking for the sea? Were they living in the sewers like those alligators in New York? Joe Doyle swore he read it in a book that one time it rained fishes in America. Millions of them.

I heard all this later but, that morning, I was in no mood to be worrying about eels. I'd been twisting and turning half the night and when I got up, the kids were like dogs. Normally they're not too bad, but it was like they knew there was something on my mind and were determined to make it worse. The kitchen was like a pigsty. Cornflakes plastered to the table, blobs on jam on the floor, cups and saucers all over the place. And the six of them racing around screaming for their clothes. She said I was stone mad to be bringing them at all, but I insisted, and at exactly ten-past-eight, I loaded them into the car and off we went.

When I saw the crowd, my first thought was that there must've been an accident.

"Snakes!" one of the kids screamed and, sure enough, slithering across the road was a shoal or a school or whatever you call it of eels. Hundreds of them.

"God, they're horrible, turn back!"

"Will you stop!"

The Guards arrived and tried to move the traffic, but they were at nothing. Men, women and children with sacks, bags, rakes, buckets and shovels, were swarming all over the place. It was like a gold rush. I kept blowing the horn until some smartass gave me the fingers. She told me not to be making a show of myself in public. She always does that.

A lad I knew to see rode by with a load of them squirming on the carrier. This teenager grabbed one and ran after him, swinging it like a lasso. Joe Bergin's wife was picking them up and, I swear to God, stuffing them straight into her handbag. The kids were delighted, but I was like a lunatic, beating the wheel, roaring at them to shut up. She, of course, flew into me again.

"Look at those gobshites running around like mice, and you're telling me to control myself."

"There's no need to shout."

"Haven't I enough on my mind already? It's easy for you to talk," and I shot her a look that would have broken glass.

"What do you call a Somali with buck teeth?"

"Joe, that's not nice."

"What is it, Joe? Whisper."

"A rake."

"Joe!"

"Will ye shut up!"

It was half-an-hour before the traffic eventually got moving. By the time we reached Ballybrittas, I had calmed down, but then she went and asked if I was nervous, and I was up to ninety again.

Between Kildare and Newbridge, I tried to recall all the times we'd made love. I had to give up after six or seven and that made me feel guilty. You make love to someone you love God knows how many times – two or three, say, in a good week multiplied by fifty-two, multiplied by eleven – and all you can remember is a blur. Then I had a vision of Archimedes counting every grain of sand in the universe, and I didn't feel too bad.

When we passed the shopping centre, the racket started up again so, just to shut them up, I promised we'd go in on the way home. I knew I'd hardly be up to traipsing around, but sometimes you'll do anything just for a bit of peace and quiet.

According to the Chinese philosophy of Taoism, during spring, men should limit themselves to just two ejaculations per week, falling to once a week in summer and once every three weeks in autumn. In winter, ejaculation should be avoided as much as possible.

"The diplodocus was the longest."

"How long was he, Joe?"

"His tail was fourteen metres."

"Is he extinct?"

Suddenly it dawned on me why I had insisted on bringing them. An unconscious need to prove to myself that I had done my bit for the propagation of the species. They were living proof that I had done my duty. Look, your honour, six of them.

We pulled into the hospital car park.

"Is Daddy sick, Mammy?"

"He's visiting an old friend of his who's very sick."

"Is he going to die?"

"Can we go too?"

"No!"

I leaned across and kissed her. They were even more surprised when I patted their heads and, one after the other, caressed their cheeks. I wanted to kiss them too, but I knew the two eldest would tell me to get lost.

I found the room. Seated opposite the door was an old woman clutching a straw bag. Was I in the right place at all? Beside her sat a fellow my own age with a blaze of red hair. I noticed that his knees were knocking. I took a seat next to two others who nodded gravely as I passed. I was in the right place. I knew by the way they were sitting, eyes glued to hands folded on their laps.

"Good morning."

The chirpy voice made me jump. She beckoned me to her desk and I couldn't believe how natural she was. You'd think I had the flu. I suppose it must have been the nerves because, all of a sudden, I was bursting for a pee. They talk about actors having perfect comic timing, but what happened next could never have been scripted.

RECEPTIONIST: Here are your bottles. It's all explained on the leaflet.

ME: Thanks very much. Where's the bathroom, please?

RECEPTIONIST: No sir, not now! One after sixteen weeks, the other two weeks later. It's all on this leaflet...

I did my best to walk casually to the bathroom. I couldn't resist the temptation, so I checked the door again and had one last look. I had to admit that I'd done a brilliant job with the razor. As I ran my fingers over the unfamiliar smoothness, I saw my mother cleaning out a turkey, heard her knife sawing through the gizzard.

Back in the waiting room, I tried to read the leaflet but the words wouldn't lie down. I looked up and found three new faces staring back at me. One belonged to a huge bull of a man with a hairy dewlap and trousers hitched above his shanks. What was he doing in this place of subtlety and stealth? I was imagining a fearsome pizzle rampaging through the countryside, a stud book nailed inside a cottage door, when he smiled timidly and between us passed a warm fraternal glow.

The receptionist called my name – Did she have to be so loud? Could she not have given me a number? – and I followed her along the corridor. She knocked on a door and smiled 'there's no need to be nervous'. The room reeked of aftershave and I pictured a line of men, their hands nervous fig leaves over organs specially manicured for the occasion.

As he gave me the anaesthetic, he chatted about the Grand National. Despite all I'd read about the vas deferens, nothing had prepared me for the shock that it seemed to be made of wire. Lying flat on my back, how could I see anything at all? I didn't need to. From the way he gritted his teeth, I could imagine what he was doing to me. With one foot on the couch, he was arched backwards, straining like a docker, pulling my dormant vas.

As I scribbled out the cheque, he said I might be sore for a few days, a week at the most. Then he led me to the door, reminded me about the bottles and wished me a safe journey.

One tablespoonful of semen contains the nutritional equivalent of two pieces of steak, ten eggs, six oranges and two lemons.

There was murder in the car. Honest to God, they were swinging out of each other. Why didn't I have the job done years ago? She told them to be good and looked at me with a tenderness I hadn't seen in years.

"How is he?"

"Grand, but he's lost a bit of weight alright."

"You're sure he's alright?"

Why the hell did I bring them? One of the most

important days of my life, and there we were gibbering in code. We were still ten miles from Newbridge when they started 'better value beats them all'.

"Will ye stop!"

I was alright as long as I could keep the legs apart, but there's only so much space between the accelerator and the clutch. I twisted this way and that, but it was no use: I had to stop and let her drive. I experimented with every sort of posture until I felt comfortable, but Buddah himself couldn't maintain the lotus position in the front seat of a Lada.

When we got there, she wanted me to stay in the car.

"What? Sit here, locked in like an oul' wan, waiting to be brought an ice cream? I'm telling you, I'm grand."

As we trooped across the car park like the Trapp family, I felt a sudden, what you might call, stirring in the loins. I hadn't expected the anaesthetic to wear off so quickly, but I consoled myself by thinking one, two, three, four, four-and-a-half, the middle of September.

"Are you sure you're ok? Look at the way you're walking."

I suppose I did look a bit odd, mooching along with my legs spread like a gunfighter, but people are good; they'd think I had some sort of handicap. For the first time in my life, women opened doors and stood back to let me enter.

"What's wrong with Daddy?"

"He has a verruca."

"A what?"

"The stegosaurus walks like that."

"Will ye stop!"

Vasectomy and shopping. It's not as rare a combination as you might imagine, for no sooner were we inside than I discovered that I wasn't alone in killing two birds with the one stone. Creeping towards us, leaning on the trolley like a walking frame, was the hairy fellow from the surgery. I was going to offer some sign of recognition – 'A snip at the price, what?' – but we passed each other without so much as a nod. I turned around to find him turned around looking straight at me. Then who should come shuffling through the aisles, supported by the old woman, but your man with the red hair.

Is there, I remember wondering, some mystical bond between vasectomy and shopping? An atavistic urge to compensate for something lost by stocking up with food? Is that why eunuchs are always fat? And what about opera singers? God knows, but my abiding image of that afternoon is the three of us shuffling like arthritic Chaplins between the beans and loaves of bread.

As we turned into the Market Square, she remembered that we needed milk for the morning. Coming out of the shop, she stopped suddenly and, though I could hear nothing with the uproar in the back, I knew by the shape of her mouth that she was screaming. I struggled out and followed the direction of her outstretched arm. Draped across the kerb, cut in two by a passing car, lay the remains of a solitary eel.

THE DEAD WALL

I

The history of aviation is a propeller shrieking in his head; a blade that lacerates the past into a million random cells. But sometimes the mayhem shudders to a halt, and words – each one a hammerblow on metal – fill the darkened room.

"The first aeroplane flight lasted twelve seconds."

Blankets stir on the floor. A young woman rubs her eyes and folds the outstretched arms.

"Oh Daddy, what am I to do? Shush now, I'm right here beside you."

Damn you Paul Larkin. Damn you for saying it. Damn you for being right. She kisses his forehead and returns to the mattress; watches in horror as the arms unfold into silent, rigid wings.

Φ

"Now, you're all set to face the day."

She props him against the pillows and, cursing the voice in her head, the voice that sneers *USELESS. USELESS. USELESS*, points around the room.

"Look, there's all your books. Look, I brought them all, every single one. They're not in order yet, but I'm going to

31

fix them up. I'll have them exactly the way you like them. And look, I have a surprise for you. What do you think?"

Stepping into the middle of the room, she sashays like a little girl.

"What do you think, Daddy? Does the colour suit me? I was very lucky to get it. It was the last one in the store."

USELESS. USELESS. USELESS.

Φ

"I'll just say hello for a minute. How are you, Liam? Are you not yourself? Are you not sleeping? Sure I'm as bad myself. Twisting and turning half the night, praying for the bit of light through the curtains."

"The Boeing 747 can carry five hundred passengers."

"Don't be fretting yourself, it's only me, Josie. Would you not stick in his arms? He'll catch his death of the cold."

"I told you before…"

"Still, if anyone walked in… Do you know what I have for you, Liam? A bit of news. I met the new curate after mass and he said he'd drop in… Wouldn't you pity him all the same, lying there like a corpse. I wonder does he ever notice us at all, or is he just remembering? Did I ever tell you about the first day he arrived?

"You did."

"He had digs with Mrs. Hargroves down by the Dead Wall. Me and your Mammy were coming up Coote Street when he asked for directions to the library. Even then, he was a woeful man for the books. Your Mammy was the lucky girl. He had his pick of the town. It was the night of the Nurses' Dance. Toby Bannan's orchestra was playing a foxtrot when he walked across the floor and, to tell the truth, I thought it was for myself he was coming. Every eye in the place was on them. You'd swear they were royalty."

"The De Havilland Comet was the world's first jet

airliner."

"Would you not stick in his hands?"

"He's not cold."

"And a year later he took her to the altar. Did she ever tell you how he proposed to her?"

"The longer we lived in the States, the more she spoke about the past."

"Isn't it a wonder all the same that he never brought her back for a bit of a holiday, and all belonging to her here? Anyway, where was I? It was New Year's Eve, and the three of us were going up to the statue for the rosary. That used to be a great occasion… the accordion band, the whole works. Outside Turpin's, didn't he go down on one knee and pop the question. Just like that. I thought he was only codding, or maybe he had a few drinks, but Tessie was grinning like the cat that got the cream. I told him to get up out of that and not be making a stook of himself in public. And the next Saturday, didn't they go to Dublin and come back with the ring."

"He was always very romantic."

"When ye came along he was so proud he used to wheel the pram himself. Where did he find the time for all that studying? The head always stuck in a book. He even used to read them to ye. I used to say would you not try something they might understand, a nursery rhyme or a little song? Then he'd start into this lecture… the glory that was Greece, the… the…"

"Grandeur that was Rome."

"That's it. The glory that was Greece, the grandeur that was Rome. Tessie never minded him at all. She used to leave him at it and come up to me. But wasn't she lucky all the same? Not many men would sit at home under two young ones."

"In May 1932, Amelia Earhart became the first woman

to fly solo across the Atlantic."

"It's OK, Daddy, I'm right here beside you."

"And then he took ye all off to America. What came over him at all? Hadn't he great prospects here?"

"The college made him a wonderful offer. I guess he just saw a brighter future in the States… Josie, I need to get some groceries. Would you mind sitting with him a while?"

"Of course I wouldn't. You go on and take your time…"

"Is she looking after you at all? I know she means well, but you'd be better off in Shaen or Mountmellick. And she'd want to start minding herself too. She's got as cross as a bag of cats. I couldn't believe it the morning I walked in and saw the mattress. I suppose all the traipsing up and down the stairs was wearing her out, but still… she'd want to watch herself or, one of these days, she'll go out like–"

"The first ever non-stop flight around the world took ninety-four hours and one minute."

Φ

"I came to apologise. I don't know what came over me. I was just… so disappointed."

"You were horny."

"Please, Catherine, I didn't mean it."

"You said what this whole damn town is thinking. Listen, Paul, do you take me for a fool? You make a pass at me, and when I'm not interested you… you insult my father."

"I didn't mean it. It's only that… I just thought we had something."

"What is 'something'? We've known each other a couple of months. You come to visit, take me out to dinner once. Is that 'something'?"

"But when you kissed me…"

"So that's it? I was… it was… a moment of weakness. No, a gesture of gratitude… a way of saying that I do appreciate the support you've given me. And you tried to take advantage of that."

"You shouldn't have kissed me."

"What? I say thanks for something and you accuse me of trying to seduce you. Is that what you wanted in return for kindness?"

"How is he today?"

"Do you need to ask? He's exactly what you called him. Will you hurry off home to write about that?"

"Please, Catherine..."

"Won't that impress your literary friends? I can hear them already. 'Paul is so sensitive. He writes with such compassion'."

"I think I'd better go. I only came to apologise."

"Has the Muse descended already? Do you have to rush away and get it down before it's gone? Go on then, back to your garret. Or is it your drawing room? I can see you... our local genius... our Man of Letters... reclining on his couch like... Oscar fucking Wilde!

"I don't deserve this."

"You make me sick. This town makes me sick. He makes me sick. My own father makes me sick. I threw everything away. My career, my friends, my whole life... to care for him. Do I deserve that?

Φ

"They told me that a cop had to pull you away from her. Is that true, Daddy? Did a cop drag you away? What was in your mind as the ambulance raced to Mount Sinai? They say that when you're drowning, your past flashes before you in an instant. Does the same thing happen when someone you love is dying in your arms? Does your life together flash before you? Did that happen to you, Daddy? The first evening by the Dead Wall? The Nurses' Dance? What were you thinking as she lay on the sidewalk? How you'd tell me? How we'd contact Michael? Is that what you were thinking? Please, I need to know. Do you remember the hospital, Daddy? Kneeling beside her bed, screaming at those flowers on the window. 'Look at them, Tess, they're still alive! Those damn flowers are still alive!' Then you started to laugh. I'll never forget that, Daddy. I'll never forget the way you laughed."

Φ

"Do you mind me asking, but how long is he like this?"

"Almost a year. The morning after my mother died, we got the news about my brother. He was living in Florida. On the way home for the funeral, his plane crashed right after take-off. His... his body was never found."

"I'm so sorry."

"When I told Daddy, he didn't say a word. Just went to his room, and no matter how I pleaded, he just screamed at me to go away, that he had nothing left to live for anymore."

"The door was open…"

"Good morning, Mrs. Carter."

"Morning, Father."

"Josie."

"Our parish priest came over, but he still refused to leave his room. Someone from the college stayed with him and when I got back, he never mentioned Mom or Michael. Just asked for those books."

"Books?"

"Books about aeroplanes, the history of aviation. I tried to talk about the funeral, but he just covered his ears and said how much he needed those books.

"That's all he ever says, Father. Oul' gibberish about airplanes."

"Please, Josie... Eventually, his friend agreed to go to

the library and, when he returned, Daddy shouted at us to go away, that he had work to do. When I looked in again, he was exactly like you see him now. Over the next few months, he was taken to different hospitals, seen by every kind of specialist. But it was no use. They could find no organic disorder. They were all agreed on that, but I've lost count of the other reasons they put forward. Catalepsy. Catatonia. Post-trauma stress... or was it post-stress trauma? I can't remember. He just withdrew into himself. There was nothing left for us in the States. I hoped that bringing him home might have some effect on him. Even after so long. I guess I was really hoping for a miracle."

USELESS. USELESS. USELESS.

"I'm sorry, Father, I never offered you anything."

"No thank you, Catherine. Don't trouble yourself."

"Please, Father?"

"A cup of tea would be lovely then. Thank you very much."

"I won't be a minute... I've just remembered I'm out of milk. I'll just step across the street"

"Please, don't bother.."

"Sure she'll back in no time at all... You can't beat a nice cup of tea. I could never take to the coffee at all. Especially the decapitated. It gives me woeful migraine."

"Isn't she a wonderful person, Mrs. Carter?"

"Her poor mother was the same. Waited on himself hand and foot. Is that the door...?"

"Miss Mangan–"

"What's wrong, Catherine, you're as white as a sheet!"

"There is no such thing as useless information! *Ipsa scientia potestas est! Mensa mensa mensam.*"

"Are you unwell? Would you like to sit down? Can we get you something?

"*Ipsa scientia potestas est!*"

"Look at her mouth, Father... her eyes...What's come over her at all?"

"Should we call a doctor?"

"Go away, go away!"

"Maybe we should call the doctor?"

"I said go away!"

"Maybe– "

"Go away!"

"Come along, Mrs. Carter, we can–"

"She's not herself, Father."

"Close that door! Damn you! Close that door!"

"In Kitty Hawk, North–"

"Stop it! Stop it! Oh Daddy, it should have been you. It should have been you... Oh, Mike, Mike."

She takes a pillow and presses it to his face. The rigid wings shudder for an instant.

"It should've been you, Daddy, do you hear me, it should've been you..."

With all her strength, she leans on the pillow until silence fills the room like darkness.

II

She examines the paperweight as if it were a precious stone, then holds it to her eyes.

"I can't see you. I can't see anything at all. Just like the Dead Wall."

With a bang that makes his papers jump, she drops it on the desk. Her eyes dart to the clock.

"When is he coming?"

"It won't be long now. He should be here any minute. How are you today?"

"Fine."

"Still sleeping well?"

"I sleep fine. When is he coming?"

"Soon now, very soon. Yesterday, you mentioned your games. Can you tell me more about them?"

"They started before we went to America."

"You were obviously very young?"

"Three, maybe four. He used to put fruit – apples, oranges, bananas – in a heap on the kitchen table. We had to close our eyes and sort them out. He was so proud when we got it right. And Mom used to stand there with tears in her eyes. Not crying, just tears."

"Did she ever join in your games?"

"No."

"Why was that?"

"He wouldn't let her. She used to buy us things but he threw them in the garbage. Said they weren't *tactile* enough. Where is he? He should be here by now. Something must have happened."

"It won't be long now. Can you remember anything else?"

"Later, he placed a stopwatch on the table to see who would finish first... Then there were the men."

"Men? You were painting?"

"Drawing. He used to get so mad when I left something out. Mike's were always perfect. Five perfect toes, five perfect fingers. He stood over us and wrote everything down. When we were done, he spent hours studying that notebook."

Footsteps halt outside the door. Catherine runs to open it.

"Oh Mike, are you OK? I was afraid you weren't coming."

"I'm fine, Cathy, just fine."

"Good afternoon, Mr. Mangan."

"Good afternoon, Doctor."

"Please, take a seat."

"Oh Mike, I miss you so much. Are you sure you're OK?"

"Honestly Cathy, I'm fine."

"You're well settled in by now?"

"The hotel is fine. I've been walking through the town, doing some 'exploring'. Places she used to talk about. The white statue, the monument. That amazing wall by the railroad."

"The Dead Wall."

"*Dead* Wall?"

"According to local legend, someone jumped from it years ago..."

"That's where she saw him first."

"Who? Catherine?"

"That's where he met Mom. At the Dead Wall."

"I never knew that...

"Mike, you look so much better now. You looked so sad that morning."

"You had never been back before?"

"No, none of us had. But when the train pulled in, I was amazed by how much I could remember. The metal bridge, the wind blowing along the platform, the church spire across the rooftops. When I found the house, it felt... I don't know... spooky. I stood in the street, waiting for... the courage to knock the door."

"Something happened when I saw you. Everything he did came back to me. The wall was gone."

"It's a phenomenon known as repressed memory. Typically, a response to events which involve death, or physical or sexual abuse. Events which destroy an idealised image of some loved one. In simple terms, the mind refuses to accept that something terrible has happened."

"But why was it only Cathy who was... affected? We

both suffered the same."

"I honestly can't answer that. But it may be related to the fact that you... got away. In other words, you accepted what happened and dealt with it in your own way."

"And Cathy didn't?"

"Precisely. Your life in New York... your experiences with your father... her mind simply blocked them out."

"And when I saw you that morning…"

"A classic case of recall. Broadly speaking, three factors can trigger the recall of a repressed memory. Therapy. Anniversaries. Similar events, sights or experiences. When Cathy saw you, something, so to speak, clicked, and she remembered everything she had repressed for years."

"It seem so simple, so straightforward."

"Perhaps, but it's an area we're only beginning to have a fuller understanding of."

"What is there to understand? He destroyed our lives! And he destroyed Mom too. She said nothing for years, but it all built up inside her... She was cleaning the den and knocked over some of his papers. I saw her crawling around the floor, trying to pick them up. I saw him standing in the doorway, screaming: 'Why are you doing this to me!'"

"Please, Cathy, don't upset yourself."

"What do you know? You have no idea. No idea about anything. You were with that tramp in Florida, so what do you know?

"Please, Catherine–"

"He stormed out of the apartment and left her crying on the floor. She ran after him... I tried to stop her... She collapsed on the street and died on the way to Mount Sinai...

"Would you like to rest for a while?"

"No, Doctor. I'm fine… He seemed to change so much in New York. It wasn't a game anymore. In First Grade we had to study dictionaries. Can you imagine that? And Mom just sat there, watching us with tears in her eyes. Too afraid to say anything."

"She was weak."

"That's not fair, Mike."

"She never tried to stop him. I hated those tears. I hated her weakness. That's why I didn't come to the funeral. I despised her, that's why. And it was a way of getting back at him, a way of making him suffer all the more."

"You're wrong, Mike, she always loved you... When we couldn't say the words, he locked us in our rooms and took away the light bulbs. When we were older, seven or eight, I guess, he taught us Latin and Greek. He used to wake us at dawn. He said our brains were more receptive then. *Mensa, mensa, mensam. Alpha, Beta, Gamma, Delta...* He was always much harder on Mike."

"Was there a particular reason for this?"

"Mike was so much like him."

"I guess I just absorbed things faster. Or maybe I was just more scared than Cathy."

"He hated you because he saw that you were brilliant too, that eventually you would surpass him."

"What I could never figure out was the paradox, the contradiction. He wanted us to be 'brilliant', yet, when we did show signs of exceptional achievement, he seemed to hate us all the more. When he wasn't preparing us – that's what he called it, 'preparing' us – there had to be complete silence while he wrote in those notebooks."

"We couldn't watch TV or bring friends home."

"That's right. Remember Tara? She was Cathy's best friend and he stopped her calling to the house. 'Inferior material' he called her. Inferior material."

"Was he ever violent to your mother?"

"He had no need to be. She was already terrified of him. Terrified of her love for him, terrified of his–"

"Craziness."

"She thought he was crazy?"

"He was. Icarus."

"Sorry, Catherine, I didn't catch that."

"Icarus."

"I don't understand."

"That was years later. We were on vacation in the Catskills. A colleague of his had a cabin there. Do you remember, Cathy? One morning, it was still dark, he woke us and said he wanted to show us something."

"He brought us to the edge of a cliff and made us look down."

"We were still half-asleep."

"*Why are you afraid? What have I taught you? There is no such thing as... Say it!*"

"*There is no such thing as useless information.*"

"*Every thought that passes... Say it, say it!*"

"*Every thought that passes through my mind is sacred.*"

"*Ipsa scientia... Say it! Say it!*"

"*You're hurting me, Daddy. Ipsa scientia potestas est.*"

"*With the gift of knowledge you can fly. On the wings of knowledge you are Icarus, borne above the ignorance of the world. You are Icarus, soaring from the snares of ignorance. Why are you afraid? Have I not given you the wings of knowledge?*"

"*Please, Daddy.*"

"We never told anyone. Even when we were old enough to realise that there was something wrong with him. He was at his worst when we had examinations. If we didn't get the highest grades..."

"Wasn't there anyone... a teacher, a friend, a neighbour... anyone you could talk to?"

"We agreed not to."

"You agreed not to tell anyone? Why?"

"We were too scared."

"No, Mike, because we loved him."

"I meant to ask you this earlier, Michael. When did you finally leave home?"

"After everything else, it was weird really... that such a simple thing, a complete misunderstanding, finally gave me the guts, the courage to get away."

"Mike graduated *summa cum laude* and we were so excited. We all were, except him."

"He just shook my hand – like he was greeting someone at a funeral – and turned into his den."

"That night, I heard Mike crying in his room. I went in and lay beside him. When he found us in the morning, he woke Mom and pushed her in before him, accusing us of terrible things."

"I know I said I hated her, but, that morning, I felt so sorry for her. She looked so helpless... so old... trembling in her nightdress. If Cathy hadn't come between us, I swear I would have killed him."

"Then he became so calm, so composed, smiling in the doorway, the kind of smile that said: go ahead, do your damnedest..."

"And that was the last time I saw him until I arrived here."

"He deserved to die. I should have done it years ago."

"How did he react to Michael going away?"

"Unless someone asked, he never mentioned him. Then he said that he was living overseas. It seems impossible to believe that everything could have been so normal, but it was."

"How did your mother take it?"

"She took his side completely. My father's, I mean. What a terrible thing it was for any child to threaten his own father... Mike looked so sad standing in the rain that morning. My heart jumped and I saw... I saw everything that happened."

He's not coming! Do you hear me? Mike's not coming. He's never coming home. His own mother and he won't be coming home. All because of you. Why won't you listen? I know why. That's it, isn't it? You know what you've done to us, and soon everyone else will too, because I'm calling the police. Right now. Do you hear me? I'm calling the police.

"But how could I..? My own father... how could I do it?

AN EXPERT ON EVERYTHING

He bought the pyjamas because he had a premonition. That's what he called it. A premonition. We were looking around the sale in Shaws when, all of a sudden, he said I'll be back in a minute and disappeared into the men's department. When he came back, he showed me this baby-blue pyjamas with a navy collar and a crest on the breast pocket and said I bought it because I had a premonition.

I had to laugh because, in forty years of married life, only once did he ever wear a stitch to bed. Only the once. And that was the night Fluffy and the tomcat were bawling on the window. He got up and rapped the window a few times, but sure they were only laughing at him. Eventually he jumped out, threw on his shirt and trousers, and tore out the door, roaring and shouting like a lunatic. He was so cold when he came back that he got in the way he was. That was the only night he ever wore a stitch. Even in the middle of winter, when I'd be wrapped up like the Michelin Man he wouldn't wear a stitch. He said it wasn't healthy, that your skin couldn't breathe properly. Then he'd start on about dermis and epidermis, sensory fibres, lymphatic vessels. I was worse to open my mouth. It just got him going. He was an expert on everything.

In the beginning I used to say will you not be talking

nonsense, but I was wasting my breath. There was no stopping him. Dermis, epidermis, sensory fibres, lymphatic vessels. Anyway, other things about him annoyed me more. I could make a list of his stupidity. A list as long as my arm. The way he pulled the stalks off tomatoes before he weighed them. The stupid way he had of saying things. If something was broken, he just couldn't say that. It had to be 'gone wallop'. And if we were driving anywhere he'd say 'Wind up that glass, I'll catch my death of cold'. Why couldn't he just say window like everybody else? No, he had to be different. I used to be mortified going anywhere in the car, but he'd say how many do you know that drive around in a vintage vehicle? How many do you know, says I, that have to sit in an ashtray on wheels?

But worst of all was the way he hated music. Not just the modern stuff or opera. All his life, he hated any sort of music. Even birds. He used to say 'will you send out the cat, how can I relax with all that squawking in the garden'? Even when I'd be trying to sing Michael to sleep, he'd tell me to shut up. 'You'll damage the ossicles that transmit the movements of the eardrum to the cochlea.' Ossicles! I was only singing to my baby. It's not natural. How could you love a man that didn't like music? But I did. Day in, day out for forty years.

I couldn't even sing in the house. When I heard him at the front door, I had to turn off the wireless or the CD player Michael got me for Christmas. But he could be funny too. Like the time he told me about your man in Clonminam that got the prescription for the pessaries. Did they work? the doctor asked. No good at all, doctor, I might as well be sticking them up me arse. And funny cruel too. Years ago, Josie dropped in to wish us a Happy Christmas and she started codding him about the mistletoe. 'Missus Carter', says he, 'I wouldn't kiss you under an anaesthetic'.

He was only happy when he was miserable. One year I succeeded in dragging him to Salthill for a fortnight. The sun was splitting the trees but there he was in that black suit. Would you not put on a bit of colour? says I, you're like a parish priest on his holidays. Off he trotted and left me to walk the length of the prom on my own.

Sometimes I thought that maybe there was something wrong with him... that maybe he'd go like the nephew or the sister... rambling the lanes, talking to the ditches. They had a few acres out in Clonad and when the Council took a bit to widen the road, she went haywire altogether. Half the town saw what happened but no-one ever said a word, and Father Pat kept it out of the papers.

The other night, I put on a CD and sat there with my eyes closed, singing along with the words. I never felt so happy. It was like I was miles away from everything. *I love you because you understand, dear, every single thing I try to do.* I could feel him slouched there in the other chair, staring at the newspaper. Then I turned the music up so loud the yoke was hopping off the table. I could hardly bear it myself, but there wasn't a blink out of him. I don't know why I did it. I just did. I felt a bit sorry after, when I thought about him just staring at the paper, but sure what harm was in it?

Do you know what Michelle asked me one night? 'What squawks and flies into cliffs?' 'A seagull,' says I. 'No. Guess again,' and she starts giggling into her hands. 'I give up. What is it?' 'Jim Reeves.' I know he put her up to it because he was laughing for ages at the good of it.

One year, for our anniversary, I made him bring me to *Kimberley Jim.* I should have known better. Things were going grand until poor Jim opened his mouth. He started shifting around in the seat, then up goes the hood of his anorak and he sits there like an Eskimo staring at a hole in the ice. And in the hotel after, he was like one of them hear-no-evil monkeys. But when he got a few drinks in him, up he gets and starts roaring at the band. I was mortified. 'Why don't ye play a solo? So low we can't hear ye!'

When Michael was a baby and he started crying, he used to go into him in his pelt. I told him it wasn't right, and he launched into this sermon about how we were all beautiful in the eyes of God; how Adam and Eve used to go around in their skins; that it was only our own bad thoughts that made us wear clothes at all. He could be so high and mighty sometimes.

Look at me. Crying again. It's the same every single day. One minute I'm laughing at something he said years ago; the next, tears are rolling down my face. Then I think of something else and I'm alright again. Like the night he got up to Michael, and when he didn't bring him back to our bed, I went in to see what he was at, and there he was, naked as the day he was born, rocking the end of the cot and counting 2366, 2367, 2368...

Do you know what I saw once on the telly? There's this worm somewhere in Africa and do you know where it lives? In a rhinocerous's tears. That's the only place you'll find it. Living in a rhinocerous's tears. Or was it... What do you call that big yoke in Africa with the bird on its back?

When I asked him what he meant, he said it again. I bought it because I had a premonition. I said maybe you're going to take up Judo and he wasn't a bit amused. I kept at him till he said he had this terrible feeling that he was going to die in his sleep. He was standing there, waiting for me to pay for the eiderdown, when he had this vision of himself lying dead in the bed and me trying to wake him up. What would you do then, he said, and not a stitch in the house for when the doctor, the priest, or a neighbour came in? And that's why he bought the pyjamas. Because he had a premonition. I said will you go on out of that, you were never a day sick in your life.

Imagine not wanting to look at your own husband. I used to love him. I really did. Sometimes when we'd be watching the news or eating the dinner, I'd stare at him till he asked me what I was gawking at. Some days now, I don't even feel sorry for him. I know it's terrible but I don't. If he tried to touch me, I'd go as stiff as a board. I want to be nice to him, but I just can't. Even when he starts to cry, it would be the easiest thing in the world to put my arms around him, but I can't. Father Pat keeps telling me that in his heart he's still the same, but he's not. I do all I can for him, and I know he's as fond of me as ever, but he's not the man I married. He's not the man that wept with happiness every night on our honeymoon. He's not the man that cried himself to sleep the night I wouldn't talk to him for calling me a bitch.

He was stone mad about Michelle. One evening, I smelt fags off her and threatened to tell Michael. His Lordship, of course, stood up for her and made all sorts of excuses. Wasn't she after coming from the pictures and the place full of smoke? When I reminded him that smoking was banned, he just laughed it off. For an intelligent man, he could be as thick as a ditch sometimes. She could have announced that she was expecting twins and he'd find some good in it. But maybe it was hard to blame him. She was like the daughter he always wanted. He loved Michael, of course, but I knew he was heartbroken when I couldn't have another. She was mad about him too. Grandad this, Grandad that. I was lucky to get a look-in at all. Still, she gave me a CD every Christmas and a card she made herself. He kept his on the locker till I said, for God's sake, it's the middle of July. To Grandad, with all my love, Michelle. XXX.

A premonition. That's what he called it. I knew what it meant, but one night, just for pig iron, I said I'd look it up. Previous warning, notice or information. Anticipation of an event without conscious reason.

Michael needed the break. He was looking woeful pale for ages, but I can't understand what he wanted with Venice. If it's water he wanted, God knows there's enough of that here. I was only too happy to oblige when he asked us to mind her. He, of course, was delighted. Off he trots down the town and arrives back with a load of comics, enough sweets to feed an orphanage, and a pair of slippers in the shape of bunny rabbits. I reminded him that she was nearly sixteen, but sure I might as well be talking to the wall. I nearly died when I caught him up on the step ladder, plastering the room with posters of pop stars. He even wanted to take out the holy water font, but I drew the line at that. I know it's dry for years, but still.

I often wonder what's going through his mind. But I'd feel stupid tapping my forehead like he was mental or, worse still, writing it down. That's what they suggested in the hospital. But I'd feel stupid. What Are You Thinking Of? A Penny For Your Thoughts? I'd love to see him smile again, even if it's not a real smile. I was going to tell him about your man from Coote Street in the hotel in Dublin – 'Would you like a serviette, sir?' 'No thanks, Miss, I'm as full as a tick.' – but I'd be all day writing it down.

The minute she came in that night, I knew she was at the fags again. I could smell the mints off her. He, of course, wanted to know if she had a cold, would she like a Disprin or a hot water bottle in the bed. She wasn't a bit happy when I said it was Good Friday tomorrow and we'd all be going to kiss the cross. As she closed the bedroom door, I'm sure she said kiss my arse. I lie awake at night and that keeps drumming in my ear. Kiss my arse. Kiss my arse.

He wasn't in great form today. I couldn't get him to stir from the fire and, when ten o'clock came, he didn't even want to go for his walk. I know it's hard, but he has to face the world sometime. He can't go on living like an owl.

I wasn't too worried about his hands, but I hated the way the doctors looked from one to the other when I said maybe he could grow a beard. I wouldn't have asked if I didn't love him. 'You don't seem to understand the gravity of the situation,' says your man with the mole on his nose. Did he think I was a real stook altogether? My husband propped up in the bed, black as the ace of spades, and he quizzing me about 'the gravity of the situation'.

Everyone says he's the image of himself, but they're all liars. Sometimes when he's asleep, I rub my finger along his cheek and it's like touching glass. I ask God to make me like him again, but it's no use. I worry about him sitting so near the fire, but I'm afraid to say anything in case there's a row. I know it's stupid but I can't stop thinking about the night I left the plastic bucket on the hob. I got him the terminal underwear in Shaws, but do you think he'd even try it on? Not a bit of it. Twisting and turning, grunting like a baby. I knew by his eyes what was going through his mind. *Is she that ashamed of me? Is she that ashamed?*

Sometimes I think that maybe he's better off the way he is... the town gone to the dogs... cornerboys out all hours of the day and night. Foreigners waltzing in for the dole... jumping the queue in the Post Office. And you'd be afraid of your life to stir outside the front door with them flying up and down the footpath. And where are the Guards? A young lad snatched Josie's handbag when she tripped over one of those bricks on the Main Street and do you think there was any sign of a Guard? Only for your man in the shoe shop she'd be lying there still...

Little do we know what's waiting around the corner. All over the world, this very minute, there's millions drinking their last cup of tea, kissing their children goodnight for the last time. We did the same thing every night for forty years. He checked all the doors and windows and I went back again to make sure the cooker was off and the guard in front of the fire. Then we said the rosary. It was a Thursday so it was his turn to give it out.

When we were getting in, I said are you ever going to wear that pyjamas? It's on that radiator since the day you bought it. Goodnight, he said, just to shut me up. I gave him his goodnight kiss and turned over. I was dreaming of Michael sailing along in one of those cornettos when he shook me awake. He jumped out and put on the pyjamas and, before I could say a word, I smelt the smoke. I tried to follow him down the hall, but I must have passed out, because the next thing I knew I was in the hospital and all I could say was Oh God, what am I going to say to Michael?

FLAGS

"Sir! Sir! The cops are after getting Peter's Daddy!"

"They took him off to jail!"

"I was coming back after lunch and I seen them at the lorry!"

"Hold on now, hold on. What's all this, about?"

"The Guards and the soldiers were outside Murphy's."

"A load of them! Guns and jeeps and all!"

"And Jack Murphy was in the squad!"

I could see him moving about the packed pub, the papers folded over one arm… standing outside the prison, the misspelt placard on his shoulder… the mornings Peter handed me the unsigned homework and mumbled about Mammy being busy and Daddy down the country with the calves. The Easter Lily. The night he took him to the Wolfe Tones. *Come out ye Black and Tans* in the corridor next morning…

The bell rang. Pushing through a riot of speculation, I urged them inside.

"Peter isn't back, sir."

"The cops–"

"*Ciúnas anois*! We'll see tomorrow."

That evening, the strange familiarity of local names filled the kitchen. The television voices – arms and ammunition, murder of retired judge, man assisting with enquiries – somehow seemed remote but, for hours afterwards, my head swam with all sorts of images. His hand pumping mine at First Communion. The same hand dripping unsuspecting blood. A bored child, his eyes suddenly alive for a favourite history lesson. Pearse staring sideways. Connolly in a chair. Calves. Straw. Guns. That rough hand squeezing mine in welcome, the stubbled face telling me he knew my father.

Φ

He was coming in each day as if nothing had happened, his homework neatly signed by his mother or some visiting relation, and I found myself responding with uncalled-for compliments, exaggerated smiles. Before long, he even began to boast about his visits to the prison, but the others soon lost interest in his tales and preferred to distract me with Culture Club and Michael Jackson.

One morning I was shocked into accepting from his outstretched palm a wooden pencil case ablaze with harps and shamrocks, flags and swords of light.

"Daddy made this for you. He made it all himself."

I mumbled something in Irish, sent him back to his seat, and left the gift behind a pile of books on my desk.

Afraid of showing sympathy? Of somehow 'supporting the Cause'? You who sneered at rebel songs, read Pearse's poetry to prove he was a pervert. But fled to the bar when he approached your table with An Phoblacht. *For God's sake, it's only a harmless present from a child.*

When the bell rang, he swaggered to the toilets and, through the open door, just loud enough for me to hear, came the customary jibes:

"Teacher's pet!"

"Suck!"

Next day he was back at my desk again, this time leaving two crumpled bits of paper on the Roll Book.

"Someone keeps throwing these at me."

JACK MURPHY KILLED A MAN.

Jesus.

PETER LOVES THE PROVOS.

"They're always at me. The whole class. In the yard and after school when you're gone home. Mammy says you're to put a stop to it."

I bit my lip and read the words again. Pens scratched to a halt. Ears were cocked.

"Alright, Peter. *Suigh síos anois.*"

Avoiding his smug, expectant gaze, I held up the bits of paper.

"Who knows anything about this?"

"About what, sir?"

A fly buzzed in the blind and somewhere in the building a toilet flushed.

"Now look, I won't ask again… Alright, someone's telling lies. Take out your jotters. One hundred times tonight…"

"Ah, sir…"

"I MUST NOT BE DISHONEST IN CLASS."

Tearful with disgust, his eyes met mine, lingered for a moment, then stared intently at the picture of the Pope above the blackboard.

Next morning, the pencil case was gone from the press I'd put it in the day before. Of course I knew what had happened, but for some obscure reason – pity, relief, spite? – I decided to say nothing and when I turned and saw his seat empty I wasn't all surprised.

It was still empty the following morning and, although I thought of him on and off throughout the day, by three o'clock, Peter Murphy was just another absent child. I was locking up when footsteps clattered through the corridor.

"Sir! Sir! The cops are outside!"

The lake lies halfway between the school and the Murphy farmhouse. At the water's edge, a neighbour held Mrs. Murphy in her arms and as I approached, her eyes bore a hole right through me. In the corner of my eye a frogman zipped his suit. One of the Guards said something, but I just stood there, staring straight ahead at the pencil case bobbing on the surface. *Daddy made this for you. He made it all himself.* Mrs. Murphy started to wail again when, all of a sudden, Peter burst from the trees behind us, his laughter more terrible than any scream.

BANISHED CHILDREN

He cut the paper into identical rectangles. On one he drew a tiny matchstick man; on another a broad inverted V. A room full of hooded prams floated through his mind and he drew a semi-circle perched on two smaller spheres. On the fourth rectangle he drew a spindly £ and finally, a crude pirate's flag.

Three or four times that first night, he rose to check the bolted door, stood for a moment listening to the sounds from Coote Street but otherwise, never left the table. Over and over again, he examined each rectangle; sometimes trimming the edges, sometimes darkening the lines. Occasionally he swore and crumpled one of them, then waited until it floated up the chimney like a black leaf. But mostly he just sat there, staring at nothing, thinking about his life and those who had abandoned him. When he began to feel tired, he cleared the table, swept the floor, and watched until the flames took every scrap away.

He took the five rectangles, closed his eyes, blessed himself and threw them in the air. Shivering with excitement, he knelt and groped around the kitchen floor. He counted to five, opened his eyes and gazed at the pirate's flag. It was to be the Week of Bones.

Gathering the other pieces, he stuffed them into the

pillow. He lay on the bed, the black missal in his hands, and thought about the night he stole it from Sister Majella's office. Opening a page at random, his lips followed the Latin in a soft phonetic crawl. When he reached the end of the page, he ripped it out, tore it down the middle and continued until his chest was dotted with tiny bits of paper. He opened a second page but soon fell asleep, the missal clamped before him like a crucifix in the fingers of a corpse.

Φ

First he made a list of names. A list spanning his life in the town. Girls who sniggered when he approached them in the Macra; children who mocked his garbled tongue; local men who, he always felt, bore some resemblance to himself. Women he liked the look of. Finally townspeople at random. He found addresses in the phonebook and, over and over until the letters swam before him, he checked his scrawled columns. Suddenly recalling their funerals, he cursed under his breath and scratched out different names.

He took a bundle of newspapers from the wardrobe, stood and listened intently, then, pulling on a pair of rubber gloves, began to cut up the headlines. He worked until the scissors hurt his fingers, then collected all the letters. Everything else went carefully to the fire. He fell asleep with the missal in his hands and dreamed of a yard full of shivering boys. Steam billowing from the laundry. He saw himself peering through the forbidden workroom window; the thick clothy smell; the rows of timid girls, their scissors a swarm of silver insects.

Φ

After Mass on Sunday, he dropped letters into five different postboxes. He spent Tuesday evening in the Hare and Hound, mooching about the bar, nodding to faces he knew, his ears alert for any sign. He did the same on Wednesday, and when he overheard 'Did yours come this morning too?', the drink trembled in his hand. Before going to bed that night, he threw four rectangles in the air and the pram decreed the Week of Holy Angels. He dreamed of the desert. He saw an infant, its arms and legs hysterical, its mouth a crimson O howling at the sky. He tried to follow footsteps fading to infinity. He saw snakes sliding from the sand into a room of sleeping children. He saw them winding through the bars of his cot: felt beads of fire lacerate the dark. He saw a man and a woman's face, their gargoyle laughter pressed against the window.

Φ

The third card decreed the Week of Mothers: cutting, pasting, writing, he worked as feverishly as before.

Φ

Hoc est enim corpus meum…

As the host was elevated, he tested the words and tried to match them with the sounds he'd made from the missal. His eyes wandered from the altar to the stained glass window. He gazed at the tableau of saints and angels until it dissolved into the body of a woman. But, no matter how he tried, turning the image round and round in his head, he could not catch a glimpse of her face. Outside, he strolled among the congregation, but heard not a whisper of anything extraordinary. He wondered if something had gone wrong.

Φ

On the night he was preparing for the Week of Pounds, the local sergeant sat opposite the parish priest. Strewn between them on a walnut table were the letters he had sent. They selected pages and like card players glanced at each other for reaction. They passed them back and forth until the priest had read the last one. The clock ticked louder as the sergeant shuffled them from hand to hand.

"Did you notice anything, Father?"

"The spelling? The postmarks?"

"Apart from that, look..."

With grave deliberation, he divided the sheets into three lots.

"Now..."

"These are all the same... all to do with death and dying."

The policeman handed him another lot.

"Children. God save us, how could anyone..."

Again a grave nod and an arm extended across the table.

"Disgusting, Father. All addressed to women."

"Out and out depravity. Who could think, let alone write such things?"

For the next hour, they discussed the townspeople who had come to see them.

"Maybe it's only a prank, some sort of sick joke?"

"Whatever it is, it's an abomination. The whole town is talking."

Φ

"It is, my beloved brethren, the work of the Devil himself. Satan has come amongst us and entered the soul of whoever is responsible for these terrible acts. Let us be vigilant, let no stone remain unturned until this sower of dissent, this vile perpetrator of division, this disseminator of calumny and detraction is finally brought to light..."

Φ

"Yours are all the same?"

"Identical. All to do with money."

"Such appalling accusations ..."

"They're getting very angry... wondering what I'm doing to stop it."

"Do you think I haven't heard them too? They have a path beaten to this door. Have you nothing to go on, nothing at all?"

"Not a whisper, Father."

Φ

On his way to and from work, he stopped at the bridge and gazed into the river. Savouring the worst obscenities he could think of, he closed his eyes and saw a man showing his son how to hold the rod, how to scoop a net beneath the surface. Passing the forest, he heard them again, felt the child's squeals of laughter as his father mimicked different birds.

Φ

On Saturday evening, the priest's housekeeper found him on the doorstep, offering her a sheet of paper as if it were a bunch of flowers. She looked at him sideways and ushered him into the parlour. As the priest read the letter, he could feel the eyes directed at his own. You got them too, God help you, he thought grimly, and recalled the timid child in Holy Angels; the first morning he drove the nervous teenager to the factory. He remembered the times he came upon him in the empty church; his innocent confessions; the evening he met him by the river, his pockets full of stones. As if talking to himself, the priest continued: 'I can't understand it at all... the whole town in a ferment... rumours flying up and down, old secrets, dead and buried for years. The most disgusting accusations. God knows where it's all going to end... people afraid to go out at night... old friends at each other's throats...'

That night, while the town slept, he worked until his fingers pained him, cutting letters from the newspaper, pasting them on to fifty single sheets. Early the next morning, he walked to the station and waited for the next train to Dublin. He wandered the streets, dropping envelopes into every postbox he met. He arrived home exhausted and, for the first time in many years, fell asleep without the missal.

Φ

His matchstick man, the V, the pram, the £, the flag: there they were, on the front page of the *Leinster*. His whole body trembled as he mouthed the headline: MYSTERIOUS REQUEST. TOWNSPEOPLE TO ASSEMBLE? They were doing it for him. They were doing it because they loved him.

He washed and shaved, brilliantined his hair and, like a priest vesting for the altar, put on his Sunday suit. As he locked the door, he could hear the voices in the Square. *To thee do we cry, poor banished children of Eve, to thee do we send up our sighs, mourning and weeping in this valley of tears.* From T.C. Kelly's gateway he stood and watched them; his people, his family, united by love, gathered there to greet him. They were there because they loved him. As the churchbell struck five, their prayers intensified against the darkening sky, calling to him, beseeching his forgiveness.

THE GREATEST LIVING POET

"Surely you don't mean–"

"I do."

"Mr. Murphy! I can't believe this! Emo... Togher... Our beloved local–"

"Knock them all. Think of the starving millions. All the coffins you could make, instead of planting them in rags."

I was prepared to leave it at that, but she launched into this sermon about poems are made by fools like me but only God could make a tree.

"Exactly. Now you're talking. Do you know what trees are? They're arrows. Arrows fired by God to keep us in our place. Everywhere we turn, we're hemmed in by trees. They're a symbol, a metaphor for mankind's lack of free will."

The bitch gazed right through me, at the rent-a-crowd, the clink of sponsored glasses.

"Prison bars. A stockade to keep us from seeing beyond our own little patch. And another thing. Did you ever feel the urge to get up on a tree? A big strong oak or chestnut?"

"Certainly not. Why should I do such a thing?"

"Because they're phallic symbols."

"Disgusting!"

"And did you ever collect conkers?"

"Please, Mr. Murphy, be serious."

"Of course you did. And do you know why?"

"Mr. Murphy, I really don't think—"

"It's a manifestation of every woman's desire to emasculate a man."

"You drunkard. You pervert. You... gatecrasher!"

Sure I was only trying to rise her. The things that come into your head. Is it possible to have a single second with nothing happening, an instant when your brain is as barren as a skull? I'll find out. Quiet please. Dim the lights. Experiment No. 1. 5-4-3-2-1...

I am spellbound as Aladdin rubs his lamp. A magnesium flash, an explosion of my breath, and he is gone behind a swirl of smoke. Slowly it dawns on us that something has gone wrong. The Genie bursts from the wings and kneels over Aladdin who twists in agony on the floor. His hands clutch his eyes. 'I can't see! I can't see!' Along the Main Street, past the courthouse, the barber's window slick with haircuts from the Fifties, comes the tapping of his stick. Black glasses hide the pantomime of terror in his eyes.

No, it can't be done. Experiment deemed a failure. Maybe it's possible for Joe Soap, but definitely not for a poet. A poet's head, a true poet's head, is different. It is a foundry, an armoury working non-stop day and night. In the white heat of suffering, words are sharpened into spears. A poet's head is the forge of confrontation. Poor Timmy. Thirty years rubbing that lamp behind his eyes. The things that come into your head.

Main Street. A grey-haired woman fumbles in her handbag. Scented gloves, tickets for 'Aladdin' in the Worsted Mills, a prayer book full of memory cards.

Ro-ock, rock-a-hula baby. What am I at lying here in the cold? Get up, get up. What's that? Shit. The bottle's in bits. Let that be a lesson for you. Never trust the pockets of a sports coat. Mind the glass. Too late... Look, we're blood brothers, him and me. What am I saying? I'm not like that bastard. Look, I am Padre Pio, the patron saint of poetry! Trees. That's why I thought of the reception. I am surrounded by trees. I run for miles, the clothes plastered to my back, and I end up surrounded by the prongs of God.

Where's your poetry now?

Listen. Even the wind in the trees. Laughing at the poet.

Coffins for rags! Coffins for rags! Write about that, write about that.

"Ye won't be laughing come Christmas!"

Look what they've done to me, down on all fours, panting like a dog. Look. Snow. Even God is spitting at the poet. What's that up ahead? Still there. Get up, get up. Jesus, my legs have a mind of their own. A shed. Locked. The bastards have it locked. Do they think they can do this to a poet? Do they think they can silence me with their puny slings and arrows? Mind your eyes with that glass. Coming through! Fire in the hole! I hope the drink hasn't ruined the matches.

Drums of fuel, chainsaws, a pickaxe. God bless the happy woodsman. Ha ha ye philistines, I'll tear ye limb from limb, slash your tyres, make crystals of your searchlights. The agony of bones, the laughter of the chainsaw. Look out, ye bastards, here I come, the Kenwood Chef of Poetry.

The Old Chapel. The Men's Confraternity. My father singing out of tune at Benediction.

Wait till I get out of this jacket. Jesus, that's sweat... is that blood? There it is... good old Crested Ten. Three cheers for John Jameson. Up Cork. C'mon the rebels. Look, the pariah poet, gnawing every drop of goodness from the pocket. You ain't nothin' but a hound dog. A foundry. Did I say that? I'm ashamed of myself. Cheese-and-wine poetry. It's a miracle I haven't lost the bag. Where's the matches? The memory card. Her First Communion picture. Mind the blood! Look at those eyes. They could be mine. Her poor eyes could be mine. Five years writing to the Minister. Five years crying before Councillors and TDs. But I sorted them out. If you're looking down on me now, Mammy, you'll see, I sorted them out. By Jesus, I got revenge. The house never the same. Day and night as sad a place as Lourdes. The half ring. What could I do? She came at me like a disease. Love me tender, love me true.

The Electric Cinema. Elvis close enough to kiss. Jack-the-Lamp prowls the aisle, a walking-stick of light beside him.

The things that come into your head. What's next? Spin the wheel. Fingers on the buzzer. Come on down! Are you ready, words? Start walkin'!

A report has just come in that a man has been found dead in the maximum security wing of Portlaoise prison.

Poor Daddy. The things that come into your head. How did I end up in here? Was I drawn by some atavistic memory? Did one of my people flee here after 1798, yeoman blood still glistening on his pike? Who fears to speak of '98? I'll tell you one thing. That bastard will never speak again. Did Mammy's people set lime for birds, scrabble in the dirt during the blackest days of '47?

Rock-a-hula baby. Only for me the whole town'd be gone. That's the pocket done for. The sleeve should keep me going until they find me; dogs, lights, megaphones screaming through the dark. Let them come. I am ready. Let them drag me by the hair, rip me to pieces. True poets are born to die. While I'm waiting, I might as well be thinking. List, in alphabetical order, ten things that must be suffered by the poet.

Absence. From a Daddy who died for Ireland.

B is for... Banality. A good one. Banality.

Compulsory Purchase Orders.

Destruction. Of the landmarks of youth, the lifeblood of art.

Evenings. Staring at the four walls.

Friends. None.

G... G... I'll think of something later.

Home. H is for Home

I... Invisible? No. Inability. That's it. Inability to procure a regular supply of Crested Ten.

Φ

"If you ask me, he was always a bit of a bollocks. Poncing around with that nancyboy bag, spouting about poems and the trans... the whatdidhecallit?"

"The transsomething power of words."

"The power of words me arse. When did poems ever buy a pint?"

"Or pick the winner of the 3.30 at Lincoln. Meself and the lads'd be waiting for the results and we'd watch him through the window. Sticking up poems, handing out them bits of paper. One word on every page. You could hear him roaring on the Curragh. 'Come together, people of the Midlands, unriddle the spinks of life! Throw away the baubles of banality!' I ask you, what sort of carry-on is that? Bawling about fucking bananas. In broad daylight?"

"And what about the banger?"

"The Kingmobile? Sure he drove that into a ditch years ago. Going home one night in the horrors."

"He was as bad in school. Remember how he used to go on about Elvis? The Bard of Memphis. The greatest living poet. Stop the lights!"

"Remember the night of the concert? 'I'd like to recite a poem about repression in the modern world' and he starts into 'You can knock me down, step on my face.' Give us a break."

"I was stuck beside him for two years in the Tech and it

was the luck of God he didn't get me thrown out. Remember your man, the baldy bollocks with the wig?"

"Tintawn."

"That's him. Tintawn. He came into the class like a bulldog, and what did the eejit do but admit everything straight away."

"You were worse to have anything to do with him. Sure weren't they all half-mad. Look at the oul' lad... the spirit of 1916. Some fucking spirit alright, planting bombs in a pram. And wasn't the mother locked up for years?"

"He paid me. Half-a-dollar a go. My job was to plant the incendiaries. That's what he called them, incendiaries. The idea was that some oul' wan would open a love story or a cookery book and it would explode in her face. Still beats me how a poem could fucking explode, but there you are, that's the way he was."

"Who gives a fiddler's about poetry anyway? Especially the women. No wonder he could never shift."

"Another night we were up in the Wild Turkey when in he waltzed with the handbag on his arm."

"I wonder is he a bit bent?"

"I wouldn't put it past him. Anyway, there was great gallery when Bobo swiped the bag and we fucked it around the floor. Bits of paper flying in all directions. It was like a fucking wedding. And what did the bollocks do but start to cry. I swear to God, in front of all the lads, lepping up and down in the air, crawling around on his hands and knees bawling like a woman, and we all going where's your mammy gone, chirpy chirpy cheep cheep."

Φ

The first duty of the true poet is to publish nothing. Once polluted by ink the magic disappears. The second is: be ruthless with your gift. I unleash words into the darkness, a virus to contaminate your sleep. I invent ways to give the bourgeoisie insomnia. That is my posterity, not some timid little pamphlet oohed and aahed at by the Arts Council and spinsters up in Dublin. My poetry is the phone screeching in the dead of night.

The things that come into your head. Listen, what's that? Sssshhh, listen. No. Just a rabbit or a fox. He must've got a whiff of the Crested Ten. Tally-ho hark away me boys away.

I wonder have they found him yet? I was only doing my duty. That's all. Doing my duty like Elvis in 1958. Private 53310761. The bastard deserved it. Didn't he destroy Mammy? The Main Street, the chapel. Even the Kingmobile. I'm sorry, Mr. Murphy, but under the Road Traffic Act… Road traffic! I gave him traffic. An eye for an eye, a tooth for a tooth. That's what the bible says. An eye for an eye.

Φ

Of course I'd heard all about him too, but there's two sides to every story. I used to see him in the library or sitting on his own in Egan's, and he was the most harmless looking creature in the world. To tell the truth, he was very good-looking. Even the girls – and they believed every badminded whisper in the street – had to admit that much. The morning he bumped into me at Fortune's corner he couldn't apologise enough. At the time I didn't notice the smell of drink but I remembered it later on. When I met him again he invited me for coffee, and the minute he sat in front of me, I fancied him like mad. I know it sounds stupid… I didn't know whether to laugh or cry when he told me the handbag was his mother's…

In the beginning I used to humour him, but he knew I'd rather talk about anything but poetry. And do you know why we got on so well? Because I could see that it was all an act, all looking for attention. I knew that, behind the big words, all the talk about the past, how there's an ancestry to every breath we take, all the save our planet for posterity, he was no different from the rest of us...

He could be so romantic too. Like the time he spent a fortune on the gold ring and then sawed it in half. I said are you mad? but he said that sailors used to do it years ago. He gave me one half and made me swear that no matter what happened, no matter where we ended up, we'd always be together. Another night, at the pictures, he pulled me into him and whispered I love you so much I want to inject your blood into my veins.

I felt so sorry for him living out there on his own and the place falling down around him. I thought that if I was with him every night he might go easy on the drink. I found out after that he was in every pub in the town before he called for me at all. Then I tried cooking. He'd say the meal was brilliant but he was sorry, he had to meet someone. This went on for the best part of a year: 'Honestly, I'd love to stay, but I have to meet someone.' Sometimes I wouldn't see him for weeks, then he'd turn up on the doorstep smiling like a Jehovah. I'd throw my arms around him and bring him in. We never said a word, just sat there holding hands and him crying no-one understands me, no-one understands me.

Φ

The trouble with poets is that they see poetry as a private, solitary art. Send the wife off to the pictures, tell the kids to shut up and there it is, waiting like a bowl of cornflakes on the table. Aphorism No. 1: The poet must burn the garret in his head. My poetry flourished in the daylight, grew stronger in the glare of confrontation. It took on the Council, the bastard that locked up my mother and destroyed the memories of my youth. What is a poet without the memories of his youth? Like Hitler in his bunker, he pawed the map, planted flags, and sent his henchmen to destroy the town I loved. And nothing blocked their way but poetry. While politicians, historians and Greens wrung their hands in meetings, I was on the streets, hoarse from crying in the wilderness. Only words stood between my past and the slavering curs of progress. But they were futile: pebbles hopping off Goliath's chest. But I've taught him not to tangle with a poet. *Please, Mr. Murphy, be serious.* I'll tell you one thing: she won't be so high and mighty when they find him. She'll be sorry he never put a preservation order on himself.

Query. If poetry stems from the deepest emotions, why are there no poems in praise of hatred? Of letting black babies starve to death? What's more emotional than murder? Why do only good people write poetry? Essential rules for would-be poets:

1. Wipe Africa from the map of your emotions.

2. Ditto cancer, sick children. Are you a poet or do you want to be the Rose of Tralee?

Φ

When I arrived, there was maybe half-a-dozen of them gathered round the JCB. At first I thought there must have been an accident, but then I saw the old woman, squashed into the bucket, threatening to do away with herself if they didn't give her back the field. I tried to talk to her but she wouldn't budge. After a while, the foreman ordered two lads to lift her out. In a flash she whipped out a breadknife and drew it across her arm: "Are ye happy now? What do ye think of that? Get back, get back, ye pack of bullyboys. Are ye not content with taking the bit of land? Is it blood ye want as well? I'll give ye blood. All the blood ye want!"

When the bossman appeared, she went hysterical altogether: "D'ye see this? D'ye see this? It won't be the first time a Murphy died a martyr!"

I went and called the station, but the sergeant said do nothing, let the Council sort it out themselves. So I stayed in the car. To tell the truth, I was half on her side anyway. She never had it easy what with the husband topping himself in the prison and the young lad wandering around in a world of his own.

The bossman looked at his watch and stepped forward again: "Now, Mrs. Murphy, I have the whole thing sorted out. Show me that knife like a good woman and the Council will discuss the matter at the earliest opportunity."

She threw back her head, laughed like a hyena, and stuck the knife into her leg: "D'ye take me for a real stook altogether? I want the bit of land back and I want it back this minute!"

The next thing I knew the engine was revving up. Jesus, I said to myself, they're hardly going to heel her out? But they didn't. They just left her in the bucket and the JCB headed for the road. It was pure bad luck that there was a match in the field the same evening. I can see it still. I was never so ashamed. Me out in front with the lights flashing; herself roaring 'God save Ireland! Four green fields. Give us back the bit of land!' And stretching back along the road, carloads of lads, leaning out of windows, waving flags, wondering what the hell was going on.

Thanks be to God we got rid of them at the field, but we still had to go through the town. Did you ever wish you were a dwarf? Now and then I looked in the mirror and there she was, waving the knife and bawling. By the time we got to the hospital I was sweating like a pig and I wasn't a bit sorry when they carted her inside.

Φ

What's keeping them? Has the shock nailed them to the

floor? No. They're scurrying through the offices, screaming for Form 36A. Requisition: an ambulance, a priest, four buckets of hot water, four mops, four Brillo pads extra large. Maybe they got stuck in the snow? The wind through that window is like a knife. Daddy's sports coat is in shreds. What am I going to do? I can't lie here all night. I know. I know what I'll do. I'll trudge through ice and snow, head down against the wind, along the lane, the main road, past the football field and the barracks, the swirling Square, lads full of beer pegging snowballs at Our Lady, the courthouse, Fortune's corner, until I come to Liam Ryan's: shake the snow out of my hair, march up to the bar, *howaye lads, bad night out, I put that bastard in his place, what?* put money on the counter and hold the Crested Ten like a baby to my chest. Listen... What's that..? They must've found him. Quick. Quick. Ladies and gentlemen, Elvis has left the building. Elvis has left the building.

THE QUEEN OF SHEBA

It was New Year's Eve and she was in St. Mary's watching Gerry Ryan, when he suddenly appeared beside her and asked her what she thought of 'your man'. From that very first moment, he made her feel that every word she said was interesting. The following week in The County, he whispered in her ear that his happiness depended totally on hers. And so, their life together became one bright, delirious trail of cinemas, pubs and discos.

Now, every evening was the same. He came in from work, muttered something towards the pram, washed away the smell of oil, gulped the food she had prepared and spent the hours till bedtime sorting through his records, studying a tableful of charts and magazines. Now and then he stopped to light a cigarette, leaned back in his chair and allowed her to speak to him through thick, contemptuous smoke.

The weekends were worse. He came in, showered, ate, loaded the van, fixed the banner, then disappeared for the night. In the beginning she tried to stay up, but now never saw him again until she awoke to find him sprawled beside her.

Φ

She was mixing the baby's bottle when he emerged from the

bedroom.

"You were late last night."

"Is there no milk?"

"There's a carton in the fridge. What time were you in at?"

"Sometime after twelve. Where's the sugar?"

"I was awake till after two and you weren't in then."

"So what? Doesn't the money come in handy?"

"I never see much of it. You can hardly walk into the bedroom with all that stuff you have."

"Do you think they want to see some clown with a mickey mouse system and a load of crap singles?"

"I think it's time you started to cop yourself on, started acting your age. They must have a great laugh at you, perched up there with your fancy lights and the American accent."

"I'm warning you, don't start… what American accent?"

"Don't I hear you *rehearsing* when you think I'm asleep. 'Ok Guys 'n' Dawls…"

"I don't have to listen to this."

"But you'll listen to everyone else. Does it ever cross your mind that you're a married man with a wife and child at home?"

"Jesus, where's my overalls? I'm going to work!"

As the door slammed, she put the bottle in a jug of water and began to clear the table. An advertisement in the paper suddenly caught her eye.

Saturday, October 31st. Saturday night. What am I thinking?

She checked that the baby was still sleeping, then dialled her sister's number.

If it rings five time I'll leave it.

"Mary?"

"Howaya? All well? How's Richard and Paul?"

"Not a bother, we're all grand."

Go on, ask her.

"Sorry for ringing you in work, but I won't keep you a minute. Paul's due his bottle. Listen, Mary, could you do us a favour? Richard's bringing me to Keno's on Saturday night and I was wondering if you could stay with Paul. We won't be too late?"

"No problem, what time do ye want me?"

"He has to be there early to get his stuff organised but I'll be time enough around eleven."

"That's grand, the train gets in just after ten."

"One thing though. If you happen to bump into him – he sometimes gets parts in Kildare – don't let on you know. It's supposed to be a big surprise for me but one of the lads let it slip. I'd better go, Paul's starting to stir. I'll give you all the news on Saturday"

What am I after doing? No, he deserves it. When I'm finished with him he'll be ashamed to walk down the town again.

Φ

The week had been the same as all the others; their silences broken only by words flung across the table. The house was quiet now, but it was a different sort of silence: no tension in the air, no pressure building up inside her till she felt her head would burst if she didn't do something; press her nails into her face, sweep his records off the table, scream until she wept. The terrible urge to shake the bawling child.

She waited until she heard the van rattling down the street, then went into the bedroom.

I went as red as a beetroot when he got me to try it on in the shop. It hardly covered me at all. God knows what your one thought. I was freezing out in Salthill but I never let on. He seemed so proud to be lying there beside me. Couldn't keep his hands off me in the hotel. Will it fit me at all? That lace curtain your one cut too short... the silk scarf... That's her now.

"How are you, Mary?"

"What! Jesus, is that you at all? You're like one of those ones in whatdoyoucallem... harems!"

"Well? What do you think?"

"I'll tell you one thing. You'll catch your death in that outfit. What did Richard think?"

"He said I look sexy."

"You'll be lucky if you're not arrested."

"Sure they'll all be dressed up. I'd better make a move or he'll be wondering where I am.

Φ

Nervously, she hurried down Grattan Street, her coat tight around her, hoping no-one she knew would want to stop and talk. His van was outside Fortune's. SIGHTS AND SOUNDS BY DIK'S DANCIN' DISCO. *Make sure everyone sees you alright!* Never changing her stride, she shot out an arm and, with a venom that made her grit her teeth, tore the banner to the ground.

Walking through the bar was like walking through the history of the world. Heroes, villains; real, imaginary; past, present and future, rubbed shoulders and swapped stories with cartoon characters, rock stars, peroxide icons from the Fifties, a girl she recognised from Crazy Prices trying hard to be Madonna. A fat man in a Hawaiian shirt, bristling with credit cards and cameras, offered her a drink. With hardly a glance, she snatched it and strode towards the music.

"And now Guys 'n' Dawls, an oldie but goldie, a blast from the past, a rave from the grave!"

She grimaced as a song she liked pounded through the room, then fought her way through the crowd. A man in Buddy Holly glasses and a loincloth beat his chest and roared at her to 'get down and boogie'. She turned away, straight into the arms of a teenager in a toga.

"How's she cuttin'? Are ya the Queen of Sheba or what?"

Slobbering a mouthful of grapes, he looked shocked as, violently, she pulled herself away and fixed the scarf around her face. Within yards of the stage, she stopped and stared at Richard. Silver shirt slit from throat to navel, a gold medallion twinkling on his chest. She felt her hands clench in fists of rage as her body moved in slow erotic curves, her arms gradually clearing a circle on the floor. Shimmering faces formed around her. Oblivious to any music now, she responded to the shapeless beat of memory: exotic scenes from Sunday matinees long ago, nights of bitterness and tears, blatant sex in her husband's secret magazines. She whirled around the floor, the lace a blur, her hair a taut black mane. She stopped suddenly, waited for the room to right itself, then confronted his leering gaze. Arching backwards, her legs apart, she shimmied towards the stage.

"C'mon Guys 'n' Dawls, let's hear it for the bellydancer! C'mon, let's hear it! Yowsah yowsah yowsah!"

Close enough to see the blonde hairs on his chest, she swept the scarf from her face. He leapt from the stage and reached to grab her shoulder. She squirmed from his grasp and clawed her way through the dancers, tears blinding her eyes, *Oh Paul, Paul, I'm sorry, I'm so sorry,* and ran through the bar, past the turning, startled faces, *Paul, Paul,* through the door and past the van of DIK'S DANCIN' DISCO.

ADESTE FIDELIS

Within hours of the announcement, his portrait beamed from every window in the county. Within days, teachers had drummed his favourite song into cacophonies of children. Factories worked around the clock to produce flags, mugs, tablecloths and lampshades. In Mountrath, one enterprising baker concocted a limited edition, once-in-a-lifetime, Basilica Bun. The world of Haute Couture responded with typical alacrity. White T-shirts worn with yellow jeans were flaunted on the Main Street while, in the Golf Club, two-tone albs were *de rigueur*, with lurex mitres and silver croziers as optional accessories. The same establishment reported a brisk trade in contraceptives which, upon expansion, revealed the luminous legend *Urbi et Orbi* and gave off a whiff of incense.

As the Great Day approached, travel arrangements obsessed every resident of the town. Old men, who hadn't seen the city since 1932, aired suits of clothes and dreamed of climbing Nelson's Pillar, buying a cake in Bewley's and sausages in Hafner's. As if preparing for a festival, teenagers packed rucksacks and guitars, and sewed his face on the back of denim jackets. Over pints of cider, they discussed the pros and cons of hitch hiking, in particular the advantages/disadvantages of musical instruments, miniskirts, wet T-shirts, physical deformity etc., etc. Train and bus tickets were paid for in advance. Cars were serviced, wheelchairs oiled, and bicycles pumped for what promised to be the greatest mass mobilisation in the county since the Easter Rising.

Early on the eve of the Great Day the exodus began. Like lemmings, the faithful citizens of Laois left their homes and converged upon the Phoenix Park in Dublin. Since its opening to the public by Lord Chesterfield in 1747, this vast natural arena had witnessed many strange and wonderful phenomena: the assassination of Lord Frederick Cavendish and Mr. T. H. Burke on May 6, 1882; the establishment of the racecourse in 1902; an unrecorded number of clandestine assignations resulting in early weddings, paternity suits and the nightboat to England.

But nothing would compare with the scenes anticipated on this glorious Day of Days. As the light of dawn broke over Dublin Bay, a soprano from The Swan craned her neck and warbled that the *Feis Ceoil* wasn't a patch on it at all. A Camross man spat into his hand and swore begod it was bigger than the County Final. What elicited such allusive wonderment was, in short, the sheer size of the assembly. Over acre after multicoloured acre stretched this vast weight of humanity until it seemed that the earth itself would surely start to crumble. One conservative estimate put the attendance at approximately two million. Two million! Fifty-per-cent of our blessed, chosen isle.

With many hours still to go before the Grand Arrival, the multitude never once fell prey to boredom, nor, indeed, the slightest sign of unease. Somehow, on this historic Day of Days, the wheels of private enterprise never ceased to turn and, thus, every conceivable distraction was made available to the patient throng. The packed rows were infiltrated by clowns, singers and step dancers, nimble purveyors of everything and anything from rosary beads, programmes and autographed pictures to lukewarm burgers, condoms (*Urbi et Orbi*), and KISS ME QUICK hats. In and out they threaded, these intrepid entrepreneurs, bearing sandwiches and chocolates, records and tapes (*Live at Castel Gandolfo*), folding chairs, step ladders, telescopes, periscopes, trays of slopping drinks.

At the very rear of the multitude, under the shade of towering oaks, a mobile home with an Offaly number plate was driven into position and parked. Mercedes doors purred open and six attractive ladies slinked into the caravan. Red neon flashed above the doorway – The Holy See! The Holy See! – and suddenly, as if on signal, a squad car came bouncing across the grass.

In the midday sun the stage could be viewed in all its shining glory. Ascending on all sides in lofty, tiered resplendence, its centrepiece was a white marble altar and plain wooden throne whose simplicity served only to accentuate the grandeur all around. Thousands of white-and-yellow banners stretched against the flawless sky. The formal beauty of a million flowers, the pomp and circumstance of singers and musicians all combined to conjure up a scene medieval in its majesty, a spectacle undreamt of by Cecil B. de Mille.

Suddenly a speck appeared in the distance. Children leaped, invalids creaked to their feet as it became a dragonfly hovering in the heavens. Silently, or so it seemed, such was the pandemonium of welcome, the helicopter descended, and the Great Occasion, the most wonderful event in the proud annals of Irish history, was finally at hand.

A fanfare split the air and a procession of clerics shuffled up the steps and formed a perfect crescent. Flanked by two burly prelates, The Great One stepped from the wings and approached the thicket of microphones. He adjusted his glasses, gazed upon the tumult then, raising both arms skywards, uttered his first words to the assembled Half-of-Ireland.

"*Popule Hiberniae, vos amo.*"

This endearment was greeted with such approval by the multilingual citizens of Ireland that the Observatory at Dunsink registered an upheaval of grade six on the Mercalli Scale of Felt Intensity. When the uproar finally subsided, a Laois accent cried out in response:

"*Tantum ergo adeste fidelis!*"

The Great One smiled and marvelled at the erudition of the Irish. He cleared his throat and a great silence hushed its way to the furthest corners of the field. At his shoulder, Paolo da Lira, president of *Istituto per le Opere Religiose* – commonly known as the Varican Bank – scanned the crowd with hawklike eyes and tapped a caculator.

Slowly The Great One began: "My brothers anda sisters, beloved bambini of Santo Patrizio e Santa Brigida, it gives to me a great pleasure to maka my first expedition to the Green Isle, famous for her forty shades of emerald and the faith of oura fathers. She is also famous for her musica: many time do my padres from Irlanda say to me about the musica bella of Irlanda. It is, my brothers anda sisters, about the musica that I wish to say a few little words. Beware, O my Irish children, la musica diabolica. You know what I speak? I speak the Rock anda Roll. Do you, my children of Irlanda, know what this Rock anda Roll mean? It mean how you say the relations between the woman and the man. It isa name given to the most holy of God's gifts by the negro American man. My children, I say to you again. The musica of Satan will lead you to temptation. Hear me as I beg to you... no more Rock anda Roll. There is no place in heaven for the Rock anda Roll. Also the Country anda Western. It isa not good too. This musica she teach to you the adulterio, the divorzio, the stand on youra man".

The Coolnamona Kid, in buckskin shirt and wellingtons, glares in disbelief at a youth festooned with swastikas and chains.

"Man above, did you ever hear the likes!"

"He can say what he likes about that cowboy shite, but what about the Rats?"

"Rats me eye. What about Big Tom?"

"No bleedin' eyetie's coming over here to badmouth the Rats!"

"Now I want to say about the Irish dancing. On the day of Santo Patrizio, I see on TV thisa Irish dancing and it isa not good. Young men of Irlanda should nota dress like the little girl. Many psicologi he say to me that sucha thing brings sin in later lifes. And also, it isa not good to see, how you say, cailinis, expose his higher legs. The human body isa the temple of lo Spirito Santo and should nota be exposed for all to come and see..."

"*Éist leis!*" spits An tUasal Maolseachlann Ó Rinncú, *Uachtarán, Cumann Damhsa na hÉireann*, "sure God knows you can't bate a good reel!"

"*Ná bac leis,*" his companion placates, "*Ná bac leis in aon chor.* Maybe he's getting it mixed up with Disco or them lads in the tights."

"Didn't he say he saw it on the box? It must've been during the Comhaltas tour of Europe. Well, he'd no right to say we're all queers and call the women good things. *A anam don diabhal!* What about his own crowd in the Vatican, them lads in the stripey knickers?"

"I speak next to all the parents, the father anda mother of Irlanda. In Italia there isa much making of the bambino. So much bambino he is born that il dottore he say to me that the woman she have to wait two years to be in l'ospedale materna. This isa a great blessing, because in the eye of our Heavenly Padre there isa no thing like un bambino piccolo. But in Irlanda today not so much bambino he is born. Thisa makes my two eyes to weep. Listen as I say to you, my father anda mother of Irlanda, go forth anda multiply."

"Will ya increase the Children's Allowance?"

"Now you're talking Missus, what about the mickey money?"

"Now my beloved brothers anda sisters... la letteratura. Your little country she hasa the long history of the book. In my own libreria I read the Irish message of the Sacred Heart and many libretto ofa the Catholic Fruit Society of Irlanda. This are all good reading, but out of Irlanda too there comes Giacomo Joyce. Thisa man hasa no place in the homes of Irlanda. Thisa man who came to Italia and say bad thing about my beloved Roma. Thisa man was instructed by i Gesuiti. I have no love for Giacomo Joyce. I have no love for i Gesuiti and hisa black pope. And this reminds me ofa something. I say to all the padre here today, I do nota want you wear the jeans anda coloured clothes. I do nota want the mandolino, I meana the chittara, in the house of God. I do nota want the longa hair, the drinking of vino in bettole, the amicizia with female ofa opposite sex. Alla this isa not good for the man of God. Our heavenly Maestro did nota play the mandolino.

Now I speak about the Gran Bretagna. I read much the long historia between youra countries and now, my beautiful Irish friends, I besiege you, on my bent leg I besiege you, to forgive Gran Bretagna for the sins she do to you, the invasion of Norman and his cavalieri, the murder of poora Robin Hood, Patrizio Pearse, Edmondo de Valera. Lasta year I meet with Margherita Thatcher and I tell to you, my besta Irish friends, she is una bella donna. In her heart of heart she care very deep for Irlanda."

A veil of silence descended on the assembled Half-of-

Ireland. Suddenly, from an enclave hidden in the throng, a Northern voice split the limpid air:

"Tiocfaidh ár lá! Tiocfaidh ár lá!"

Hesitantly at first, then with fierce determination, two million voices sang *A Nation Once Again*. Clearly moved by such a melodious response, The Great One removed his glasses, dabbed his eyes, then raised both arms to acknowledge the acclaim. Shock and anger ran like wildfire. Clerics eyed each other nervously as the reaction flew like missiles towards the stage. Voices that hadn't roared so loudly since the last All-Ireland hurled abuse and lewd suggestions. Sensing that something had gone badly wrong, a soldier leaped upon the rostrum and urged the Number One Army Band through a medley of *Slievenamon*, *Limerick You're a Lady*, and *The Skies O'er Ballyroan*. Enchanted by this unexpected interlude, The Great One attempted to tap his foot in time, but eventually desisted and pondered the quaint rhythmic patterns of the music of Irlanda.

"Grazie, grazie. Céad Míle Fáilte. It make me happy that you like so much my words to you. If my padre in America del Sud they listen as good, I am the happy pontiff. There isa one more thing I have to say: for many year the people of Irlanda are suffer from a terrible *pestilenza*. It is, my Irish friends, the *pestilenza* of the alcool. My bishops he say to me that all Irlanda she is covered by the alcool. Every little street isa river of the vino. In the holy name of Padre Matteo, apostle of the tenpence, in the holy name of Matteo Talbot, patron saint of thisa fair city, I aska you to stop the alcool. *Basta! Basta!* And I will tell you more. People of Irlanda who do not stop the alcool hasa no place in the *unam sanctum catholicam et apostolicam ecclesiam"*.

The effect was instantaneous. As if walls of flame had suddenly appeared behind them, the assembled Half-of-Ireland, one enormous, maddened beast, stampeded towards the stage. It kicked over chairs, loudspeakers, banners and hapless invalids. It trampled prayer books, crutches, rosary beads and burgers. Nuns fled in terror as it smashed the barriers and panoply of flags. An old man from Clondarrig, abandoned in the melée, slowly picked himself up and straightened his tie. "Holy God tonight, we'll all be arrested. I'll never get them sausages now."

THE AMAZING RESURRECTIONIST

Turn the stubborn dial of memory. Scan the years for half-remembered signals. Turn, turn. Listen. Listen close through fifty years of static. Turn, turn. A bell? Turn a hair's breadth... Yes... a bell and... footsteps. You have the sound, now close your eyes... close your eyes, let darkness bring the vision.

I knew it.

Along the Green Road he comes, past the nuns' field, the circus field, Daltons *Players Please*, the golden hands of the malthouse clock. At the Dead Wall his bell is routed by the thunder of a train.

I just knew it. The minute my back was turned off you trot down memory lane. Were you listening to me at all? What did I tell you? Memory kills imagination. You must resist it, fight the easy image, the banal voices pouring poison in your ear. Write about what you don't know. Everything else is journalese. The minute you excavate your childhood you've had it; you're just a sentimental scrawber terrified of Time. Didn't I warn you about autobiography; the mediocre details death bloats into significance. But you won't listen, so off you go...

Further up the street, the old man with the English voice and name of a Latin poet sits in a room of dust and paper, dust and thick brown light. He lays aside the sheaf of paper, rests his legal glasses on his nose, and turns just in time to catch a boy's head bobbing above the orchard wall. You can see him now, stretched along the thickest branch. You can see him on your doorstep, his red eyes begging scraps of homework. Sixpence for the unknown alphabet of algebra, the secrets locked inside the square of each right angle.

Do you know what you are? A mortician. A mortician varnishing the dead. A pretty adjective here, a nice turn of phrase there... Who's the boy? The one you tied with binder twine and forced into the stable? Flung matches through the window till the whoosh of smoke made you race across the fields? Don't embalm the past in lyricism. Give us flames. Give us screams. Give us a child praying for piss to wet the straw around him. Can you find the words for that?

From deep inside his workshop, T.C. Kelly's voice booms across the Market Square. *Testing 1, 2, 3. Testing 1, 2, 3.* By the longed-for brown guitar, the bellman passes through the Square where, far into the future of wintry summer days, the statue will refuse to move for cynic or believer. He stops to rub his shoulders, blinks at the man on the white horse, the Lone Ranger of Ballyfin, then shuffles past the voices coming from the sweet shop:

"Go on with yourself, Peter."

"I'm telling you, sure as I'm standing here fornenst you. Last Stephen's Day I seen them. Forty-nine robins frozen solid on a holly bush."

The man behind the counter is still laughing when, into the sunlight, spruce in navy overalls and tennis shoes, rides the famous German Dunne. Into Keegan's yard he veers, past the shop from the last century whose mistress was never old enough to take coppers transformed by silver paper into nervous, guilty shillings.

Past the politician's pub where the fat American blew the strangest nose a child had ever seen, then slobbered Irish whiskey and warned you with a wave of dollars to say nothing to your mother. Vying with the sound of cars, the bell alerts the narrow street. Perhaps it's never heard in the Brooklyn dream of thatch and whitewash, geraniums on the window, the old man with a nicotined moustache, but it penetrates the laneway where the blacksmith said he never hurt the horses.

It's easy isn't it, when they're all dead? What do you think you are? A magician calling them back like rabbits from a hat? Roll up! Roll up! One night only! The Amazing Resurrectionist. Bring pictures of your loved ones. Roll up! Roll up! One night only. Women and children half price. Hey presto! Abracadabra! The Fiddler Finn, his wedding suit as fresh as the night they laid him out. Look! Death jilted at the altar. Roll up! Roll up! Lazarus Lalor smiling from her shroud of words.

Down Main Street now, past the fish-and-chip shop where the confirmation boys sprawled across the table, gangsters in their double-breasted suits. He halts outside the barber's greasy profiles, scours his pockets for an inch of crumpled Afton, a box of Friendly matches. Two brothers emerge, shivering in the sunlight. He lifts his clouded face and, sniggering to each other, they run across the street. In the window of the holy picture shop they make faces at each other and the girls behind the counter. Further down the street, they rub the nose of the station horse, statuesque in blinkers as Guinness barrels are unloaded from the dray.

A small, grey-haired woman looks nervous as he spits away the butt. She appears before you now, her face a map of bones; the lightness of her body, the darkness in her eyes bringing tears for every time you broke her heart. You'd torment a saint in heaven, so you would. Torment a saint in heaven.

At the archway, a young boy sucks a liquorice pipe then wipes his fingers in his hair. It is those black lips you see today; not the chiselled features of the cinema Apache who, between the death of Challenger and the hope of Halley's comet, shocked his own children by leaving them forever without warning.

Do you leave the light on all night? Staring at nothing, pondering the immortality of stones?

The street widens into the Lower Square where once you lay in wait for showbands.

"All gone."

"Ah mister, just the one."

Sometimes, tired from nights on every stage in Ireland, they never heard your breathless cries:

"Dickie, Dickie, throw us a snap!"

Just what we need. A musical interlude. Spit on me, Dickie! What about the shed behind the dancehall? Your skin a coat of sweat, tears making anger of your lust. Where's the music in that? EGBDF. Juggle them all you like, you'll still come up with lies.

But sometimes, too, a speeding arm appears and, floating through the morning, come the stars of wireless and exotic television. Shoppers are amused to find, beaming from their baskets, a painted beehive blonde or, yodelling from the footpath, a cowgirl with a monogrammed guitar. Bouncing in their prams, babies clap their hands as five, six, seven, eight satin-suited Daddies fall laughing in their laps.

Past the Post Office he comes, between the coffin shed where you became a frightened vampire for a tanner, and the shop behind whose pagan doors, one still Good Friday evening, you scorned all childish Easter eggs and bought your first LP.

Past the pub with the name that always made you laugh – *Mr. Cryptic! Give us a clue. The suspense is killing us!* – comes the shuffling bellman. He stops and struggles from the sandwich board, then lowers himself onto one of Eddie Boylan's sacks. In the draper's porch the corner boys are jeering:

"How's she cuttin', Tommy?"

"Have ya e'er a smoke, son?"

With mischief glinting in his eyes, one of the lads bounds across the street and produces from his ear a magic wrinkled Woodbine. From Hume's doorway, someone calls 'Ay JohnJoe, Casey Dempsey's in the Macra Friday night!'

Now he faces into Bridge Street, rests, and peers into the poisoned stream, the forbidden boundary of your town. But like the school around the corner and the songs our fathers loved, his bell still travels through the ether of the years. Through years of joy; through years of pain; through years of loss and change it comes, received and finally scattered by the nighttime and the dreamless haze of sleep.

II

HOME

Portlaoise is the principal town of County Laois in the Irish midlands. The county is the only one – of 32 – with no English translation of its name. It is also, as every local schoolchild could once rattle off, the only county in Ireland that touches a county that doesn't touch the sea. The county name derives from Laoiseach Ceannmore, an ancient historical personage whose name may be translated as Laoiseach, great leader, but definitely not, as one linguistic wag with the *cúpla focal* had it, Laoiseach with the big head.

A tributary of the River Barrow, the Triogue[1] (once called the Blackwater) flows through our town and, as far back as 1999, the Environmental Protection Agency conferred on it the dubious distinction of being Ireland's fifth-most-polluted waterway.

Laois County Council's website paints an idyllic picture of our town parks: 'places of peace and tranquillity... safety and comfort... many native trees, birds and wildlife... a walkway will bring people along the edge of the River Triogue.' The path by the river in the grandly-titled River Triogue Linear Park is, in fact, (summer 2015) fringed with tall nettles, and the river itself so overgrown that it is, in places, practically invisible. It is thus a serious health and safety hazard, especially for children. Wildlife? Apart from scavenging crows and the odd butterfly, all I've ever seen there are unleashed dogs being a nuisance and a potential danger to people. But let's leave the Triogue to find its own way towards Mountmellick while we travel back the best part of half a millennium.

The town grew up around a fort established by English settlers in 1548. This was half a century before the founding of Jamestown, Virginia – which marked the beginning of English colonisation of America – so, is it any exaggeration to say that our town was the cradle of the British Empire?

The fort occupied the area where Fitzmaurice Place, Scoil Mhuire and the old Vocational School ('the Tech') stand today (January, 2016), but its only visible remains are a low circular tower and considerable portions of the wall. The fort was initially called Fort Protector in honour of the Duke of Somerset, Lord Protector of England but, in 1557, the name was changed to Maryborough in honour of Queen Mary. At the same time, Laois became known as Queen's County. In 1570 Queen Elizabeth I granted a charter of incorporation and, throughout the second half of the 16th century, Maryborough ('That town of evil omen, founded in the blood of the Irish, the triumphant centre of the first English plantation'[2]) remained the only town in the county.

During the war of 1641, it was captured by Catholic forces and, nine years later, by Oliver Cromwell's troops. In the late 1650's, with a population of 198 (150 Irish and 48 English), Maryborough was the third largest town in the county behind Mountrath (223) and Ballinakill (204).[3] In the 17th century, the town began to expand westwards from the fort, but the street plan that existed up the 1960's was laid out in the early 18th century. Throughout that period, the administrative life of the town was dominated by the burgomaster who ordained who could or could not be classed a 'freeman' (a member of the Corporation). In mid-century, Warner Westenra, Bartholomew

Gilbert and William Dawson formed a triple alliance which controlled the Corporation for sixteen years. The first two gentlemen, incidentally, alternated the office of burgomaster for more than a decade. There were about 400 electors in the town, one of whom, as a fascinating document from 1760 makes clear, would vote for 'whoever gives his wife most money'.[4]

Around the turn of the century, Maryborough had a thriving woollen industry and most houses had a loom, yet an 1833 report is a fairly damning indictment of how the town was being governed. 'The town is not lighted and many of the houses are scarcely above the class of mere thatched cabins'.[5] As is universally the case, such conditions were not allowed to interfere with profit-making by the few: the town (also spelt Maryboro, incidentally, and usually pronounced by old townies as 'Marbra') had a considerable flour industry, a soap and candle factory, a tannery and, eight times a year, a fair for 'cattle, horses, pigs and pedlery'.

Justice in those days was fairly rough indeed; according to the Assizes Record, in 1803, John Lewes was 'burned in the hand for stealing 5 shillings worth of hay'. He was lucky compared to Michael Kavanagh, sentenced to death for stealing a watch. It might be said that even he was lucky compared to the poor soul sentenced to be hanged and dissected in the County Infirmary in 1827.

In graphic evidence given to the House of Commons in 1832, Rev. Nicholas O'Connor, Parish Priest of Maryborough, stated that since he came to the town in 1816, there had been famines in 1817, 1822 and 1825. Many people, he said, were living on the yellow weeds that grew in corn; when administering the Last Sacraments he was obliged to pick the straw from the skins of the dying. In early September of 1832, there was an outbreak of cholera in the town and many of the inhabitants evacuated to Summerhill on the Stradbally Road.

Fifteen years later, at the height of the Famine ('Black 47'), fever raged in the town, but, thankfully, the population escaped the worst ravages of the cholera epidemic that struck Ireland in 1849 and 1850. Nevertheless, the Famine and its aftermath had a devastating effect on the population of Queen's County: in 1841 it was 159,930; forty years later it was more than halved to 73,124.

During the War of Independence (1919-21), the county was renamed Leix – a variant of Laois – and, following a proposal by a Sinn Féin member of Maryborough Town Commission, the town adopted the name variously spelt as Portlaoighise, Port Laoighise, or Port Laoise (all versions of the Gaelic for 'The fort of Laois'). One local historian, incidentally, attributed the change of name to 'a fit of pseudo–patriotism'.[6] It took some years for the new name to come into everyday use; the story goes that, in the late 1940's, the Superior of the local CBS 'modernised' the spelling to Portlaoise but, in 1959, Laois County Councillors were still discussing whether we were living in Maryborough or Portlaoise; Queen's County or Laois.

Throughout the 1940's, 50's and 60's, Kelly's Foundry, the Irish Worsted Mills (whose annual workers' pantomime was for many the highlight of the town's entertainment year), the Electricity Supply Board and the prison were some of the town's biggest employers. Today, the Kelly's site is occupied by the Heritage Hotel and Fitness Centre. Officially opened for business in February, 2003, the hotel continues to divide local opinion: for some, it is a grand symbol of Celtic Tiger prosperity and a great addition to the town's architecture and economy; for others it is an incongruous behemoth, its columned façade a gross example of the triumph of money over good taste. Personally, I like the building a lot.

Since 1974, the Worsted Mills building (opened in 1937) has been occupied by Eircom, but the prison still stands in its formidable grey glory. It is the prison, in fact, which defines the town of Portlaoise for many people. According to the annual report of the Irish Prison Service (2008), the cost of keeping an offender in what is the country's most secure jail was almost €270,000 per year.[7]

Following the controversial compulsory purchase of land belonging to the Meehan family – an issue still occasionally referred to by townspeople – the early 1970's saw the opening of the Link Road, subsequently named James Fintan Lalor Avenue. This development opened up a whole new industrial vista, with the arrival of Etschied, German manufacturers of stainless steel equipment, and a tennis-ball factory run by the Swedish company, Tretorn. But it was the succeeding decades that brought most change in the town. With the expansion of Lyster Square in the 1980's and the opening of Laois Shopping Centre in 1991, many natives felt that the heart had been ripped out of 'the old town'; that, bereft of family businesses and residences, Main Street would soon become a ghost town.

In August, 2004, a report by the Irish Businesses Against Litter League (IBAL) condemned the town as being 'down-at-heel', with Lyster Square being classed as the dirtiest area. Following the introduction of the ban on smoking in pubs in March of that year, cigarette butts became the most common form of litter. In all, nine areas of the town were inspected but only the exterior and interior of the Railway Station achieved an A Grade. In apparent contradiction to all this, in the same year's Tidy Towns Competition, Portlaoise's mark showed a slight increase. As our transatlantic friends might say: Go figure.

In the early years of the present century, Portlaoise saw tremendous change and, ostensibly, great prosperity: houses and apartments appeared like the proverbial mushrooms; we had a huge influx of commuters[8] attracted by the affordability of housing compared to the astronomical prices in Dublin, and large numbers of immigrants, mostly from Africa, the Baltic States and Eastern Europe. (I have heard Bridge Street referred to as 'Little Warsaw'.) In the 2002 Census, the population of the town was 12,127 (an increase of 28% on 1996 figures); in 2006, this figure had risen to 14,613, and it was estimated that by the year 2020 our town and environs would be home to 30,000 souls.

But in the midst of such boom,[9] we had our share of gloom. Serious doubts were expressed about the capacity of the sewerage and drainage systems; traffic congestion at peak times was rife, and we had a considerable drug problem. In March, 2002, at Portlaoise District Court, Judge Mary Martin warned of drug anarchy in the town if support services were not put in place.

In October, 2007, Irish Rail announced that railway bridges over the Mountrath and Mountmellick roads were by far the two most struck bridges in the entire country. The former took a total of 17 hits in the first nine months of 2007 while the latter – under which I walk a few times each day – was battered 13 times. It seemed that, despite all the signs and warnings, some drivers, in charge of forty-tonne battering rams (which I have seen forced under the bridge and nonchalantly driven off), were either illiterate, or totally heedless of the safety of others. More power to Irish Rail, therefore, for calling a spade a spade when they described truckers passing through Portlaoise as 'the dumbest in Ireland.'[10]

Real history was made on Thursday, June 28, 2007, when Portlaoise Town Council elected the first black mayor in Ireland. Since his arrival in the town as an asylum-seeker from Nigeria in 2000, Rotimi Adebari had been involved in various community and cultural organisations. He was elected Town Councillor in 2004 and, three years later, named

Person of the Year by *Exclusive* magazine in Dublin.

In November and December, our town hit the national headlines when it emerged that nine local women had been given the wrong cancer diagnosis at the General Hospital. They were initially given the all-clear, then told that they were, in fact, suffering from breast cancer. The subsequent reaction and behaviour of the Minister for Health, the Health Service Executive and the hospital itself was nothing short of scandalous. Not alone were these women never offered counselling but, unbelievably, they never even received a proper apology. Official investigations[11] of the entire sorry affair concluded that it was due to 'system failure'. *System failure*. No-one accepted any responsibility. No-one was deemed to be accountable. No-one was named or blamed. Weren't we living in a great little country?

So what was it like living in Portlaoise in 2007? We heard the usual, universal complaints from older people that the youngsters were 'gone to the dogs' and, despite the plethora of recreational activities, many teenagers were still whingeing about 'nothing to do in this dump'. As someone whose connections with the town go back generations, I have a sentimental, but not, I hope, uncritical attachment to the place: we have a Post Office that seems to have forgotten that its primary function is to look after post. Sure, you can pay bills, top up your phone, invest money, buy all sorts of envelopes and greeting cards. But you'll also have to queue – on one occasion it took me almost fifteen minutes – to buy a stamp. Is the postmaster – or whoever is in charge of staffing – blind to the plight of elderly people waiting patiently when only some of the six hatches are 'open for business'?

I recall being furious with the hospital for causing such unnecessary suffering to women who trusted it; mystified by the lack of a more visible Garda presence on the streets; amazed by how few faces I recognised on my daily wanderings around the town (at home I'm a tourist!); astounded by the amount of construction; appalled by the increased prevalence of drunkeness and loutish behaviour after closing time. But, then again, why should I expect Saturday night in Portlaoise to be any less rambunctious than Saturday night in any other town in Ireland?

I remember wondering what would happen when our so-called good times shuddered to a halt and the Celtic Tiger lay whimpering at our feet.

December, 2007. What was that? In the distance. Far away but definitely approaching... house prices falling... building workers let go. Whimpering. Getting louder by the day.

On September 25, 2008, the Central Statistics Office finally confirmed what the dogs in the street had known for ages... the Celtic Tiger was on its last legs and Ireland was now officially in recession. Between January 2008 and 2009, house prices in Portlaoise fell by up to 17% compared to about 10% nationally. In the same period, the numbers seeking unemployment benefit in the town increased by a staggering 120%.[12] No great surprise: the long queues outside the dole office told their own sorry tale.

New Year's Day, 2010. Given the dire economic situation, the shocking revelations of clerical child abuse, the greed of so many bankers, the flooding that caused such heartbreak, most Irish people seemed glad to see the back of 2009. Optimists did claim to see 'green shoots' of recovery; others were not so sure...[13]

In the midst of all this doom and gloom, there were some very positive developments. The new Leisure Centre on the Ridge Road was a great success since it opened in December, 2006, and, on the educational front, we now had two new schools: Portlaoise College (September, 2006) on the Mountrath Road, and the huge campus on the Borris Road shared by Portlaoise CBS Secondary School and *Scoil Chríost Rí*, the Presentation Convent Secondary School. The campus, which opened in September, 2010, was, at the time, the most modern educational facility in the country. Also opened in September, and located in the old Technical School building in Railway Street, Educate Together was the town's first non-denominational national school. In a country where more than 90% of primary schools are controlled by the Catholic Church,[14] this was indeed an historic and most welcome development.

October, 2010. You would need a microscope to find any 'green shoots'. In fact, given the scale of national debt, high unemployment figures, general antipathy towards an inept government, and bankers who appeared to be getting away with murder, we were in a worse state than ever. For evidence, you only had to walk around the town: empty business premises, streets deserted on weekday nights (one local publican quipped that even the tumbleweed wasn't out) and so-called 'ghost estates', of which there were 2,800 across the country. In starker terms, 23,000 new houses completed but unoccupied, and 20,000 left unfinished.[15]

December, 2010. The year began with icy cold, and ended with some of the heaviest snow and lowest temperatures in living memory. For weeks, the town and surrounding countryside looked beautiful but dangerous for drivers and pedestrians alike. We felt particularly sorry for emigrants whose journeys home for Christmas were thrown into protracted chaos. We were all dreaming of a green Christmas when temperatures suddenly rose, ice thawed, and pipes began to burst. Most of us were without running water for days (the sight of townspeople queuing at water tankers conjured up Third World images I thought I would never see in Ireland) and, in the extremely difficult weather, many saw the perfect symbol for the state our country found itself in.

After years of incompetence and stubborness, craven submission to bankers and developers, and apparent indifference to the rest of us, on December 15, the Fianna Fáil-led government was forced to accept an 85 billion euro bailout (in effect, new capital to shore up our reckless banks) from the European Union, European Central Bank, and the International Monetary Fund. This so-called 'Troika' – the latest addition to our Vocabulary of Gloom – concocted a deal that the people of Ireland, through cutbacks and tax increases, would be paying back for many years to come. It was indeed a great relief to be saying good riddance to an *annus horribilis* characterised by *The Irish Times*[16] as 'one of the lowest points in our 92-year-old democracy'.

According to the 2011 Census, Laois was the fastest growing county in Ireland. At 80,559, (40,587 men, 39,972 women) the population was up by 20% since 2006, a growth rate more than twice that of the country as a whole.[17] We also had the highest ratio of men to women, a statistic that prompted the headline LINE UP LADIES – IT'S RAINING MEN IN LAOIS.[18] But, *tógaigí go bog é, a chailíní*, closer inspection revealed that this applied to men over the age of 75. In a further breakdown of statistics released on April, 26,[19] the population of Portlaoise town was 20,145, an increase of 37.9% since 2006.

In effect, Portlaoise, and Portarlington in particular, had become commuter towns for Dublin. There were large numbers of people from Dublin and also sizable Eastern European and African communities in the town, and the overall population increase put great pressure on local schools and services. And despite a glimmer of optimisim following the election of a new coalition government in February, unemployment in the town remained rampant, and everywhere you looked there were signs of recession.

The late Jim Tynan's Kitchen and Foodhall may have been the most high-profile closure, but a walk down Main Street confirmed that it was far from being the only victim of merciless times.

January, 2012. That glimmer of optimism was well and truly smothered by the pall of gloom that still hung over the entire country. According to a survey of more than one thousand people conducted on behalf of the Samaritans,[20] more than two-thirds were worried they would not have enough money to live comfortably in 2012. Almost half of those surveyed were worried about losing their jobs or having problems finding work, while a fifth were concerned that they would lose their home.

House prices in Portlaoise had dropped dramatically since the height of the Celtic Tiger madness when the average price of a second hand three-bed-semi, for instance, was €245,000. In 2012, it could be bought for as little as €100,000.[21] The problem was, of course, that job insecurity and the absence of lending by the bailed-out banks, ensured that it was speculators, not young, first-time buyers, who were snapping up such 'bargains'.

Drunken rows and disturbances – especially on Saturday nights and Bank Holiday weekends – had become such a problem in the town that Gardaí doubled the number of officers on patrol. They also adopted a zero tolerance policy on public disorder: 'Anyone who acts the maggot,' warned Superintendent John Moloney, 'is going home with a charge sheet.'[22]

Also in June, it was announced that the Constituency Commission had cut the total number of TD's by eight to 158. It also recommended that, due to the increase in population, Counties Laois and Offaly would become, for the first time, three-seater constituencies in their own right.[23] To achieve the required population, Laois needed only a small slice of Kildare South, while Offaly needed a chunk of Tipperary.

Throughout the year, the Downtown initiative to attract business back to the 'old town' met with some success, but the number of empty premises in Main Street and the Market Square still spoke for itself. Half of the north side of the latter, for instance, was totally bereft of any business. Standing in the way of commercial progress was, of course, a futile task ('Money doesn't talk; it swears'), but, as a native of the town, I am constantly dispirited by the generic development on the 'far side' of James Fintan Lalor Avenue. The same big names, the same shelves stocked with mostly the same brands, the same production-line service. You could be shopping anywhere in the English-speaking world.

But above all else, 2012 will be remembered by the people of Portlaoise for one terrible reason. At the end of October, posters began to appear in shop windows seeking information about a missing young local woman. As rumour and speculation swirled around, a local man was taken into custody and, on November 7, her body was found just outside the town. The suspect was charged with her murder and awaited trial.[24] As Christmas approached, the thoughts of many in Portlaoise and surrounding areas were with this poor woman, her loved ones, and two families forever blighted by this terrible event.

January, 2013. Inspired by the stabilisation of the Dublin property market and the general increase in retail business over the Christmas period, there were those who believe that, after four years of austerity, 2013 would be the year when we finally 'turned the corner'.

The year got off to a strange start when it was announced that traces of horsemeat had been discovered in hamburgers. In most cases, the horse DNA – as it was euphemistically called – was of minuscule proportions, but one supermarket's burger was found to be 29% horsemeat. The upshot was (a) more than ten million burgers had be removed from supermarket shelves and destroyed and (b) a field day for the jokers: what would you like on your burger, Sir? A fiver each way in the 2.20 on the Curragh. One meat factory's claim that the DNA testing could have picked up trace elements from the air met with the response 'Yeah, Pegasus!'

On the local front, we had the usual mix of the good, bad and indifferent. Early in the year it was announced that Planning Permission had been granted for a new primary school complex at Aghnaharna to replace St. Paul's, Scoil Mhuire and Sacred Heart and, in September, Maryborough NS, *Gaelscoil Phortlaoise* and Educate Together moved to their new campus in Summerhill.

In September, Shaws relocated to Kylekiproe, a move heard by many as the death knell of the already embattled Main Street. The announcement shortly afterwards that the vacant premises would house a new, state-of-the-art library seemed to take the sting out of the situation, but whether that will restore footfall to the area remains to be seen.

The same month also saw the successful staging of the National Ploughing Championships which, over three days, brought more than 200,000 people to Ratheniska, just outside the town. Attractions included the President and Taoiseach, 1,400 trade tents, musical performances, designer clothes for dogs, art and craft displays, great weather, fashion shows, dancing, and live robotic milking. And, of course, the ploughing itself, in which 340 competitors vied for a prize fund of €18,000.[25] The event, during which an estimated €40 million changed hands, was scheduled to return to Ratheniska in 2014. Other highlights included the warm summer, the inaugural James Fintan Lalor School, the success of the

Christmas Market and – by previous standards – spectacular Christmas lights.

An almost unbelievable note was struck when, at a Medical Council inquiry in December, it emerged that a doctor who had worked in our hospital (February-April, 2009), 'didn't have a clue'. His potentially disastrous actions included reading an X-ray upside down and attempting to use a scalpel to insert a line. Apparently he was given the job because no-one else applied for it. Is that any way to run a hospital?

At the end of January, 2014, Portlaoise again made national headlines for all the wrong reasons. As revealed by a report on *Prime Time*, four infants – none of whom had any congenital abnormality or experienced any infection – died during or shortly after birth in the local hospital. The deaths – which occurred over a six year period – were the result of negligence pure and simple: failure to learn from previous errors, failure to act on signs of foetal distress, failure to properly administer the drug Syntocinon. And to add insult to injury, the unfortunate parents were then treated in a most cavalier manner by hospital authorities.[26] Needless to say, the Health Service Executive offered profound apologies and promised a review of the maternity unit. As I write this, Bob Dylan's lines are echoing in my head:

But you who philosophise disgrace and criticise all fears
Take the rag away from your face
Now ain't the time for your tears.

The new year came in exactly as the old one had gone out: gale force winds, widespread flooding and, in many parts of the country, millions of euros worth of damage. It looked as if we had been spared the worst when, on February 12, a violent storm hit the town. Much damage was done throughout the county and one family – two adults and three children – was lucky to escape with their lives when a massive tree fell on their car on the Block Road.

In the same month, the review by the Department of Health's Chief Medical Officer was a damning indictment of maternity services in our hospital which, it stated, 'cannot be regarded as safe and sustainable within current governance arrangements'. The report concluded that patients and their families had been treated 'in a poor and at times appalling manner'.[27] The upshot was that a number of medical personnel rightly faced disciplinary investigations, and a new team – under the auspices of the Coombe maternity hospital in Dublin – was seconded to run our maternity services.

And there we'll leave this scattershot history of our town, almost five hundred years after the O'Connors and O'Moores fled from English soldiers led by Sir Anthony St Leger, Lord Deputy of Ireland and Sir Edward Bellingham, his successor; almost half a millennium since the latter oversaw the construction of Fort Protector.

NOTES

1. Say 'Try-ogue' to rhyme with 'rogue'. Despite my consultations with accepted authorities (i.e., the late Flann O'Riain, and the Placenames Branch in the Department of Community, Rural and Gaeltacht Affairs), the origin of this name remains obscure. If you have any suggestions, I would love to hear from you.
2. Green, A.S. *The Making of Ireland and Its Undoing 1200-1600*. p. 288. Maunsell & Co. 1919.
3. Pender, Seamus (Editor). *A Census of Ireland Circa 1659*. Clearfield Company Inc., Baltimore. 1999.
4. *A Handlist of the Voters of Maryborough 1760*. National Library of Ireland. MS 1726.
5. Report by the Municipal Enquiry Commission. See *Parliamentary Gazetteer of Ireland*, vol. ii, p. 738.
6. *Laois Association Yearbook, 1991*. p. 15.
7. Report in *The Irish Times*. December 21, 2008.
8. A *Sunday Times* survey (August 2006) found that, after Dundalk, Drogheda, Newbridge and Athy, Portlaoise was the fifth most popular

town for commuters to Dublin.

9. According to a Bank of Ireland survey published in July 2006, Ireland was the second richest country in the world after Japan.

10. *The Irish Times*. October 2, 2007.

11. Published on March 5, 2008.

12. *The Irish Times*. February 7, 2009.

13. 'It looks as if 2010 will be only a little less challenging than 2009.' *The Irish Times* Business Review. December 31, 2009.

14. *The Irish Times*. November 17, 2010.

15. *Ibid*. October 24, 2010.

16. Monday, December 27, 2010.

17. *Ibid*. Friday, March 30, 2012.

18. *Irish Independent*. March 30, 2012.

19. *The Irish Times*. April 27, 2012.

20. *Ibid*. Thursday, January 5, 2012.

21. *The Sunday Times*. Analysis of Irish property values. January 15, 2012.

22. *Leinster Express*. June 13, 2012.

23. *The Irish Times*. June 22, 2012.

24. In May 2014, he was sentenced to life in prison for her murder.

25. Facts and figures from the *Leinster Express Ploughing Spectacular* supplement. October 1, 2013.

26. Minister for Health James Reilly spoke of 'the dehumanising nature of the way some people were dealt with' and how it was 'totally unacceptable' that people were not informed that investigations had been carried out. *The Irish Times* February 1, 2014.

27. *The Irish Times*, March 1 and 2, 2014.

WHEN IS A SQUARE NOT A SQUARE?

When it's the Market Square, Portlaoise. Imagine you can levitate. There you are, floating high above the town. Look down. You will see immediately that our Square is not a square at all, but an arrowhead, with Grattan Street its perfect shaft. In fact, look at the Square from any angle you like and it will never be a square. Almost an equilateral triangle perhaps, but definitely not a square.

On August 30, 1731, William Lawler one of 'ye Bayliffs of ye Burrough de Maryburrough', announced a forth-coming Assembly[1] by fixing a notice with 'four neals and drove by an hammer' to a post in 'ye Market Place'. With the exception of a hand-drawn map from 1803[2] (which shows the area as *Street* of Maryborough), all Ordnance Survey maps before 1907 also have Market *Place*. It was only in the nineteenth century, incidentally, that what we call the Market Square today replaced the Lower Square[3] – another non-square – as the main market area.

In October, 1796, the town's governing body, the Corporation of the Borough of Maryborough, presented 'an acre of ground, rent free for ever, as a site for a church'.[4] Thus St. Peter's Church of Ireland, the most prominent feature of our Square, was built to replace the 16th century Old St. Peter's, the ivied tower of which still stands – home to rooks and pigeons – in the neglected churchyard between Church and Railway Streets. The new St. Peter's was the first building to be erected (1803-4) on the Green (Commons) of Maryborough, and remains a jewel in the town's architectural crown.

In the 18th century, the Green – an area of almost 200 acres stretching along the side of the Mountmellick Road – was used for everything from cattle grazing, horse racing and duels to hurling matches and public executions.[5] Most of this invaluable civic amenity was eventually carved up between the Parnell and Coote families, with lesser shares going to thirteen freemen. The political shenanigans that resulted in this, and similar 'iniquitous proceedings', make for sombre and infuriating reading.[6]

Over the years, what Slater's *Directory of Ireland* of 1846 described as a 'spacious Market Square with a turret and clock' has witnessed markets, fair days, political meetings and religious celebrations. Held every Thursday, the markets sold clothes, pots and pans, turf, straw, fowl and vegetables. But you'd want to be careful you weren't poisoned: at the Maryborough Petty Sessions of June, 1849, a dealer was fined for selling 'putrid and unsound meat'. This, according to the magistrates, was a 'nuisance more prevalent in Maryborough than in any other market town in Ireland'. Some colourful characters also appeared on Market Day. One such was Seequaw, a sort of dental quack who practised his art in full Red Indian regalia. Apparently, he also had a bugler stationed nearby, not for the entertainment of the masses, but to drown out his patients' screams.

Later that century, the fairs were tightly regulated by the Town Commission: in February, 1877, for instance, the following arrangements were issued: horses were to be sold only in Quality Row (Grattan Street today, but also once called Coburg Street); cattle in the Market Square; sheep on the Abbeyleix Road; pigs on the north side of Main Street from what is today Railway Street to the Triogue bridge. In the next decade, what Town Clerk George Vanston asserted was the 'best fair in the province of Leinster'[7] attracted buyers from as far away as Belfast. Fair days continued until the late 1950's. What many of the people I spoke to recalled most vividly was the smell, and the streets being hosed down afterwards. Others had stories of beasts escaping from their pens and causing havoc in the streets. I suspect that at least one of those runaways was a shaggy dog.

Weights and Measures were once a very serious issue in the town; in 1833, for instance, it was stated that 'false weights and measures are in general use, by which all classes, and particularly the poor, suffer severely'[8] and, more than half a century later, George Vanston advertised that he had supplied a 'long-felt want' by erecting in the Square a reliable weighbridge with 'a competent and trustworthy man in charge'.[9]

Daniel O'Connell visited Maryborough in 1843 and the August 19 edition of the *Freeman's Journal* carried a colourful account of the occasion. The Square and streets were densely crowded with a procession of up to two thousand members of different trades, and three hundred of the 'respectable children of the town' carrying wands with Repeal ribbons. There was music everywhere: the Tullamore Temperance Band and at least seven others in their 'gorgeous and appropriate uniforms' formed 'one of the most magnificent sights the eye could behold'. But the paper's correspondent also spotted that it wasn't all spectacle and adulation, and promised to reveal more in the next issue about 'the four drunken Orangemen and the seven ugly women who menaced the Liberator as he passed through...'

On October 5, 1879, 20,000 tenant farmers gathered in the Square for the first of the 'monster meetings' organised by the Land League in the county. Within a year, almost every parish in the area had followed the advice of John Dillon – one of the organisation's leaders – to form a branch and meet every Sunday after mass. It's interesting that a report on another Land League meeting less than a year later noted that the presence of a 'Government reporter' from London was treated with 'the utmost courtesy'.[10]

The Town Hall[11] may have gone, but the decomm-issioned shell of the adjacent drinking trough remains, now serving as a flower box. The Metropolitan Drinking Fountain & Cattle Trough Association,[12] whose aim was 'free supplies of water for man and beast', was founded in London by two philanthropists in 1859. I don't know when 'our' trough was first erected, but there's no sign of it in a photograph of the Town Hall and Grattan Street taken in the early 1900's.[13] It may have been located elsewhere in the town, but, given that the Square was the prime location of fairs and markets, I think that is unlikely.

To honour the forthcoming Marian Year of 1954, the Men's Confraternity planned to erect the Shrine of Mary Immaculate, Mother of God. Most of the £1,500 cost was raised by selling raffle tickets and, amid what the *Leinster Express* described as 'scenes of piety and fervour never before experienced in the town', the shrine was blessed and dedicated in December, 1953. To mark the occasion, the town was 'gaily decorated with bunting and flags, while miniature shrines, tastefully illuminated, adorned practically every house' and loudspeakers relayed the unveiling ceremony throughout the town. The statue itself was made of Carrera marble and the railings were the work of local man Din Tynan, whose forge once stood at the corner of Grattan Street and Tea Lane. Decorations and lights for the occasion were sponsored by employees of the Irish Worsted Mills.

As well as being a place of private devotion, the shrine

has also been the venue of an atmospheric Midnight Rosary on New Year's Eve, and remains a popular landmark. Referring to the moving statues phenomenon which shook the country in 1985, a surviving member of the original Shrine Committee proudly proclaimed that 'ours never stirred'.[14]

Throughout the 1950's, May and Corpus Christi processions – austere carnivals of pious schoolchildren, Children of Mary, and the Men's Confraternity with their gilded banners – made their way from Church Avenue, up Main Street to congregate around the statue: all accompanied by prayers and hymns – *Tantum ergo sacramentum veneremur cernui* – broadcast from SS Peter and Paul's. The prayers, 'given out' in the church and answered by the shuffling faithful, occasionally got a bit tangled due to the delay coming through the loudspeakers, but almost everyone I spoke to – even those of a non-religious persuasion – recalled these occasions with a sense of warm nostalgia.

On April 10, 1966, an Easter Rising Golden Jubilee parade took a more circuitous route: assembly at the Garda Barracks, across the Square, down Coote Street and Station Road, past the Monument in Tower Hill, right turn into Mill View and Bridge Street, and up Main Street into the Square again. According to the local paper, the town was 'a riot of colour' and people thronged the streets to applaud the colour party, seven bands, the Knights of Malta, Civil Defence, members of the Old Laois Brigade, public representatives, and a host of other groups and organisations. Five 1916 veterans were the undoubted stars of the spectacle which culminated with the playing of the National Anthem and the reading of the Proclamation of Independence in Irish and English by Master J. Bennett of the CBS and Miss M. Green of the Presentation Convent.

Since then, the Square has seen everything: the good

(10,000 people turned out in 1980 to protest against the threatened downgrading of Portlaoise Hospital), the bad (its present status as a glorified car park), and the occasional late-night brawl. A 2008 report[15] recommended that 'car parking in the Market Square be removed or significantly reduced... that a high quality landscape design be commissioned, possibly by means of an architectural design competition, to reconfigure the space for the enjoyment of the townspeople'.

On May 22, 1776, a cow was either stolen or strayed off the Green of Maryborough.[16] The next time you're winding your way home through the Market Square after a night out, and your disquisition on the properties of a perfect square, as opposed to those of a parallelogram, trapezium or rhombus, is suddenly interrupted – *Listen! What's that? Over there, by the church. Do you not hear it?* – don't be alarmed; it is nothing more than the ghostly lowing of Mr. Robert Graves's dark-brown brindled cow.

NOTES

1. *Bye-laws and acts of the Assembly of Maryborough, 1731*. Manuscript copy held by Laois County Library. May be inspected on microfiche in the Local Studies section of the library in County Hall, Portlaoise.
2. Ms. 21. F. 18 National Library of Ireland. Reproduced in *Laois. An Environmental History* by John Feehan. The Ballykilcavan Press, Stradbally, County Laois. 1983.
3. It has been suggested that the Lower Square was originally called Buttermilk Square, but I have been unable to confirm this one way or another.
4. Report from *Commission on Municipal Corporations in Ireland*. Inquiry held in September, 1833 before John Colhoun and Henry Baldwin.
5. On Thursday April 10, 1777, for instance, Patrick McCann was, as the saying went, launched into eternity for robbing the house of William Drought Esq. 'of plate and cash to a considerable amount'. *Finn's Leinster Journal*. 22.04. 1777.
6. Was there much corruption in 18th century Maryborough? See *A Handlist of the Voters of Maryborough 1760*. MS 1726, National

Library of Ireland. The *Handlist* was printed in *Irish Historical Studies Volume 9, No. 33*. March 1954 and may be inspected in the Local Studies room in County Hall. It's an eye-opener.

7. Royal Commission on Market Rights and Tolls. Inquiry held in Maryborough, September 1888. Report published the following year.

8. Report from *Commission on Municipal Corporations in Ireland*. Note 4 above.

9. *Leinster Express*. September 4, 1896.

10. *The Irish Times*. August 18, 1880.

11. See separate chapter on Maryborough Town Hall.

12. Originally called the Metropolitan Free Drinking Fountain Association. Many troughs, identical to 'ours', can still be seen in various parts of Britain.

13. Eason Photographic Collection. National Library of Ireland.

14. Report by Seamus Dunne in the *Leinster Express*. January 1, 1994.

15. *Survey of Architectural Heritage of Portlaoise*. Compiled and recorded by Lotts Architecture and Urbanism for Laois County Council supported by the Heritage Council.

16. *Finn's Leinster Journal*. May 31, 1776.

THE GAS MEN OF MARYBOROUGH

On the evening of Thursday, January 21, 1858, the town of Maryborough, for the very first time, was lit by gas. But why did this landmark event in the town's history, this 'brilliant spectacle',[1] come as a surprise to the very Company set up to bring gas to the town? Let's go back a few years to when, so to speak, the first flame was lit...

The first piped-gas street lamps appeared in Dublin in 1825. Almost thirty years later, in November, 1854, Thomas Turpin, 'who always takes the lead in any matter for the improvement of Maryborough',[2] proposed the setting up of a joint stock company for the erection of a gasometer. The cost, including pipes throughout the town, would be £1,500, to be raised by shares of £10 each. To demonstrate his confidence in the scheme, he immediately put his name down for forty shares. Thus was born the Maryborough Gas Company and, within a month, £1,000 worth of shares were taken.

Work on the gasometer was scheduled to begin in the spring, and Mr. Turpin was confident that the town would be lit by gas[3] for the winter of 1855. The winter of 1855 and 1856 came and went and the Gas Company was still debating the venture with the Town Commission. A plan to erect the gasometer near the railway station was objected to on the grounds that vapours would be offensive to passengers,[4] and it wasn't until April, 1857 that the Commissioners finally agreed on a site (where the Macra na Feirme Hall stands today).

And so, on Thursday, June 4, the foundation stone of the Maryborough Gasometer was laid by Mr. Turpin, assisted by Mr. Lalor and Mr. Daniel from Dublin, engineer and contractor respectively. Under the foundation stone was laid a hermetically sealed bottle containing various coins, and documents with details of those involved in the venture. A small piece of artillery was discharged; there was much cheering by the large attendance from the town and surrounding districts, and a 'poetic tailor named Farrell photographed the proceedings in a song'.[5]

That evening, Mr. Daniel entertained more than thirty of the great and the good of Maryborough – all gentlemen, of course – at a sumptuous dinner in McEvoy's Hotel.[6] 'The cloth having been removed', various speeches were made and glasses raised to the Royal Family, the Lord Lieutenant, and Mr. Turpin. The festivities, including prolonged cheers and songs by Mr. Lalor and Rev. A. McDonnell, continued until midnight.

Preparations for the opening of the gasworks didn't always run so smoothly. Sales of the shares were sluggish[7]– so much so that Mr. Turpin, Parish Priest Dr. Taylor, and others, had to go around the town asking people to buy them – and it was also discovered that someone had thrown broken spoons into the pumps in an effort to disable them.

By mid-October, nearly all the main pipes had been laid, but it seemed unlikely that 'new light would be let into the ancient borough' by the promised date of November 1. It was, in fact, almost another three months before the town witnessed the 'brilliant spectacle' referred to in my opening paragraph. And that spectacle should not have happened on that night at all: the Company's intention was that, in order to honour the marriage of the Princess Royal,[8] the general lighting should not occur until Monday, January 25. But, four days early, some townspeople – including Patrick Quigley, the Town Commissioner who had provided the site for the gasometer – were 'so enthusiastically in favour of gas that they took advantage of Mr. Turpin and his staff of directors, engineer and contractor and blazed away in a flood of light'.[9] I suppose that, nowadays, we'd call that a stroke.

At dusk on January 25, many of the commercial premises, private houses and principal streets were officially illuminated. Townspeople of all ages turned out to witness the new phenomenon, but plans by some traders to light up their buildings with political emblems had to be abandoned due to high winds. An exception was the Main Street premises of Thomas Craven – Secretary of the Gas Company – which featured an illuminated crown and stars, on which 'the jealous winds had but partial influence'.[10]

At seven o'clock that night, McEvoy's Hotel was again the venue for a celebratory public banquet (unfortunately served up in the *Freeman's Journal*[11] as a 'pubic dinner') which boasted 'every variety of the season, a profusion of confectionary, a superfluity of choice wines' and the usual array of toasts and speeches. The same paper noted that the occasion was 'much enhanced by several songs sung in excellent style by members of the company'.

Over the next year or so, Mr. Turpin reported that the directors were very satisfied with progress so far; 70 gas-lights in the asylum and 29 in the gaol; the streets lit by 21 public lamps; and townspeople with meters installed in their homes (no number given) had 'expressed themselves in very satisfactory terms as to the superiority of gas over candles or oil'. According to the contract with the Town Commission, public gaslights were lit at dusk, extinguished before 11 pm, and not lit at all during a full moon.[12]

A meeting was held in September, 1859 to reach a final settlement with the contractor, Mr. Daniel. This was a less than congenial affair. A dispute had arisen over his alleged unpunctuality, his failure to purchase shares he had applied for, and the rather more serious matter of 45,000 cubic feet of gas leaking from the gasometer. The proceedings developed into a flurry of charge and countercharge, only resolved when the contractor reluctantly accepted reduced payment for his work.

Throughout its existence, the Company had its fair share of ups and downs. The breaking of public lamps, for instance, was so widespread that a reward was offered for information. In March, 1868, the *Leinster Express* published a letter from an anonymous shareholder which, in no uncertain terms, accused the Company of secrecy and being looked upon with mistrust. But most serious were the frequently strained relations between the Gas Company and the Town Commission.[13] As early as 1864, it was reported[14] that 'the directors of the Maryborough Gas Company are endeavouring to give the Town Commission every species of vicious opposition they could'. In 1870, the Company had difficulty in obtaining payment[15] from the Commission and the latter complained about the irregular and inconvenient way in which the town lamps were lit.

Six years later, matters reached a head when the Chairman and others, incensed at the Company's refusal to reply to their letters, proposed that if such 'outrageous treatment' were to continue, they would advocate that the town be lit by paraffin oil. Which, of course, never happened, but there was still dissatisfaction with the Company's performance[16] and friction between it and the Town Commission continued on and off into the new century.

By 1903, the retort bench (the construction which housed the retorts) was completely worn out and had to be replaced, and local builder William Carroll[17] was given the contract to build a new engine house and repair other buildings damaged in a recent storm. In March, 1914, the Gasworks manager wrote to the Town Clerk complaining that someone was pilfering money from the meter in the Town Hall: add to this, increased expenses, strikes,[18] and scarcity of coal, and it seemed that the new century was bringing nothing but new woes for the Company.

In March, 1920, following some public complaints about the state of lighting in the town, a well-attended meeting – presided over by Mr. P. J Meehan[19] – was held in the Town Hall to consider the feasibility of forming an Electric Light company.[20] This was surely a sign that the times were indeed changing; that the writing was beginning to appear on the wall for the Maryborough Gas Company. That writing soon loomed so large that, in May, the directors offered to sell its premises and plant for £2,841.00 to the new Maryborough Co-operative Electric Lighting Society. The offer was considered unreasonable and refused.

In 1928, the recently established Electricity Supply Board[21] started to 'wire' the town, and now there was no escaping the fact that the days of the Maryborough Gas Company were indeed numbered. One of the last shots fired in the saga of discontent between it and the Commissioners was a disagreement in 1929 over who actually owned the now-redundant lamp standards.[22] The Maryborough Gas Company went into voluntary liquidation that year, and the gasworks and auxiliary buildings were subsequently advertised for sale.

The buildings remained derelict until the 1950's when the local branch of Macra na Feirme acquired the site for a new Hall.[23] As contractor Jack Broomfield worked on the new building, the local paper marvelled at how the gasworks had been 'built like a fortress, how the chimney stack resembled the keep of a Norman castle'.[24] It went on to remark that 'many strange tanks and formations were found in the foundations'. I wonder if the workers ever came across a sealed bottle with its parchment bearing the date June 4, 1857, and the names of those long-forgotten gentlemen, the original Gas Men of Maryborough..?

NOTES

1. *Leinster Express.* January 23, 1858.
2. Described thus in the *Leinster Express.* December 2, 1854. For more information on the Turpin family see: www.portlaoisepictures.com/001turpin.htm
3. The basic process for making gas from coal changed little over the lifetime of the Company. Coal was heated in a closed tube called a retort. The gas given off was then cooled in a condenser. Coal tar and other impurities were removed before the gas was stored in the gasometer and ultimately piped throughout the town. The coal tar, incidentally, was sold for a variety of industrial and medicinal uses (in particular, the treatment of psoriasis, eczema, and other skin disorders).
4. Other sites considered were where the Memorial Park is in Millview today; near where Brown's shop now stands on the Dublin Road; and the old tanyard (the area behind the now-derelict County Hotel). The tannery is marked on an 1839 map of the town.
5. *Leinster Express.* June 6, 1857.
6. Lethean today
7. At one of the Company meetings, this exchange took place:
   Mr. Quigley: Mr. Daniel, the Contractor said he would take some shares.
   Mr. Turpin: That was before he got the contract…
   Mr. Daniel, incidentally, was later responsible for the gasworks at Ballyfin House. The works, much admired by the Lord Lieutenant when he visited the house in September, 1858, manufactured gas from peat at one-third of the cost of coal.
8. Queen Victoria's daughter, also Victoria, married Prince Frederick of Prussia, later Frederick III, Emperor of Germany and King of Prussia.
9. His shop displayed the Harp of Erin and the Star of Hope in 'jets of tremulous light'.

10. *Leinster Express.* January 30, 1858
11. January 27, 1858. The reporter on the night was the extravagantly-named Mortimer de Montmorency.
12. Years later (1902), there was a farcical misunderstanding between Company and Commission because their respective almanacs gave different dates for phases of the moon!
13. Despite the fact that so many gentlemen were members of both bodies.
14. *Leinster Express.* July 9.
15. The Company's Collector was the aptly-named Mr. Badger.
16. So much so that, in December 1890, Horace Turpin (a shareholder and director and nephew of Thomas) wrote to the paper describing the town lighting as scandalous.
17. William Carroll's legacy to the town also included classrooms in the Christian Brothers school which were officially opened in January, 1907, and the rebuilding of Odlum's Mill after the fire of 1909.
18. In January, 1919, for instance, the gasworks closed down after the workers struck for a reduction in working hours and what the Company described as an extravagant increase in wages, and an insistence on other impossible conditions. The employees distributed a pamphlet throughout the town explaining their position: the inevitable compromise was reached and the works reopened after a fortnight.
19. Member of Parliament (1913-1918), he became the first State Solicitor for Laois (1922) and County Registrar (1926).
20. In September, 1923, the Town Commission accepted a tender for thirty gaslights in the town but also, and significantly, a tender from Odlum's Mill to supply electric light to eight lamps on the Ridge, Mill Lane and the Green Road.

    The first public electric light in Ireland, incidentally, was a lamp outside the offices of the *Freeman's Journal* in Prince's Street, Dublin in 1880. In 1891, Carlow became the first provincial town to adopt electricity, but a year later, only 14 of the 103 patrons of the local gas company had adopted the new medium. (*The Gasmakers*, Charles J. O'Sullivan. Irish Gas Association/O'Brien Press, 1987. Page 144)
21. In 1929, the hydroelectric plant at Ardnacrusha was commissioned and the ESB eventually bought out all the small companies throughout the country. Thus from the early 1930's, electricity was available to anyone who wanted it in Portlaoise town.
22. The Town Commission had received enquiries from people who wanted them for sheds.
23. The Macra na Feirme Hall was officially opened on August 15, 1955.
24. *Leinster Express.* August 6, 1955.

THE TOWN'S FIRST RECORDING STAR

There is today no shortage of recorded music by local artistes.[1] But in the 1920's, the honour of being the first Maryborough man to perform internationally and have his singing released commercially belonged to the now largely and, I think, sadly forgotten Patrick Ward.

He was born on August 3, 1896, in Lyster Lane,[2] the third son of Charles[3] and Bridget (née Shea) Ward. By the time of the 1901 census, Charles, a tinsmith, originally from Birr, King's County (Offaly today) had married his second wife, Maryanne, and the household now included three sons and three daughters. Maryanne and two of the girls – aged seventeen and ten – are listed as Hawkers of Tin. The eldest lad, Thomas, was following his father's trade; his younger brothers were both scholars, and their sister Julia was only three. By 1911, Patrick also had two stepsisters, Maryanne and Josephine.

He attended the local Presentation Convent and Christian Brothers schools. According to the late local historian Patrick F. Meehan, he joined the British Army during World I and 'took part in many of the battles'.[4] After the war, he developed a deep interest in breathing exercises 'as an aid to physical perfection'[5] and, as we will see, this interest later became a major part of his life.

Mr. Meehan's article also states that, unable to find

work locally, Patrick went to England where he got a job as a porter in a London hotel. It was here that he was heard singing by the soprano Armilita Galli-Curci and she persuaded him to go to Italy to have his voice trained. His tuition fees were paid by the soprano and Guglielmo Marconi, the inventor of wireless telegraphy.[6]

Both Mr. Meehan and an anonymous obituary in the *Leinster Express*[7] refer to Ward's glittering career in the opera houses and concert halls of Europe, America and Australia, and while there are minor errors of fact, there is no reason to doubt their general accuracy. But I must query the assertion that Ward sang opposite the Irish *prima donna* Margaret Burke Sheridan in a production of *La Boheme* in La Scala in Milan. I have consulted an acknowledged La Scala expert, and also checked the details of *La Sheridan's* performances in Puccini's popular opera[8] and found no sign of Patrick Ward.

Is it possible that both obituarist and historian were confusing Ward with Thomas Burke, the tenor of Irish extraction who did appear with Burke Sheridan in *La Boheme*? Or more likely, were they confusing La Scala in Milan with the Scala theatre in London[9] where Ward did appear in 1931? They both also refer to the fact that Ward sang before King Victor Emmanuel III of Italy and the English King George V. Apparently, the former exclaimed that he couldn't believe Ward wasn't Italian; the latter announced that the whole Empire was proud of him. He also sang before Pope Pius XI but, as far as I'm aware, the pontiff's response has not been recorded.

Before I go any further, a word of caution. It seems to me that, throughout his career, Patrick Ward, in true showbusiness style, wasn't averse to self-promotion or what today we'd call hype. In one interview,[10] for instance, he claimed to have made 'hundreds of records', and worked in 'every film studio in France, Germany, Austria, California and New York'. Further research may demolish my doubts – I hope it does – but, for now, I can't escape the feeling that more than a pinch of salt is called for here. But he definitely did study in the Royal College of Music in London and, in 1924, out of an entry of more than 300, won first prize in a contest open to tenors of all nationalities. He also sang at various concerts in the city, including one, in June, 1926, in aid of Earl Haig's Appeal for Distressed ex-Service Men in Southern Ireland.[11]

His brief recording career began in May, 1927 when he recorded *Macushla* and *Dear Love, Remember Me* in London. Some months later, at a gramophone recital in a packed Theatre Royal in Dublin, *Dear Love, Remember Me* was played as a demonstration disc during a publicity campaign for Gramophone Week . Under the heading OUR LOCAL TENOR RECORDED, the *Leinster Express* praised the record and noted that 'we have received intimation from the Beltona Company that owing to the phenomenal sale of Mr. Ward's record, the first impression has been completely sold out, but a second supply will be available immediately'. If you come across *Macushla* in the attic or down behind the sideboard, I'd love to hear from you. [If you do happen to stumble on this or any very old records, remember that, presuming your turntable has the facility, they must be played at 78 rpm (and are likely to damage your stylus)].

Patrick Ward's earliest recordings were released on the Beltona label. (Richard Thompson fans among you will, no doubt, be familiar with his tribute to 'the best brand in the land'[12] which, based in Edinburgh, is still going strong today.) Ward made at least four records for Beltona. He may also have recorded for other labels in the late 1920's, but the only ones I am certain of are Ariel, Imperial and Parlophone, for which in 1928, he – excuse the 1960's terminology – cut at least ten tracks. (It was Parlophone, incidentally which released The Beatles early records and continued to do so until the band's own Apple company was founded in 1968.) Despite Ward's own estimation of his recorded output, my research would seem to indicate that it barely exceeded two dozen songs. I would love if someone can prove me wrong on this.

His career seems to have been closely followed by, in particular, the *Irish Independent*. Its issue of October 21, 1927 reported that, 'gifted with an agreeable voice which gained him a high reputation on his debut in Ireland in 1924', he was planning a concert in Dulwich in aid of ex-servicemen. According to the same article, he could sing in twelve languages and, some years later, the programme for a variety concert in the Scala theatre in London described him as 'the Irish Caruso'.[13] The obituary and the article by Mr. Meehan both mention that, as well as being one of the first Irishmen to sing on the BBC, he also appeared in films. Both sources mention *Sweet Iniscarra*, partly filmed in Laois, but now sadly lost. They also say that he sang at the Eucharistic Congress in Dublin in 1932. John McCormack's rendition of *Panis Angelicus* at High Mass in the Phoenix Park seems to have entered the national psyche but, so far, my research has not revealed any details of Patrick Ward's performance which, I have been told, took place on O'Connell Bridge.

The above-mentioned La Scala concert must have been one of his last professional stage performances because, in February, 1932, he announced[14] that he was retiring from the stage to take up teaching. He already had two studios in London and, in 1934, the following notice appeared in the *Irish Independent*:

Professor Patrick G. Ward. International Operatic Tenor and Teacher of Singing. Interviews by appointment only c/o Gresham Hotel, Dublin.

As early as 1923, he had been awarded a Teacher's Diploma at the Perfect Voice Institution of Chicago and received testimonials from various Maestros. Here's one:

> Dear Sir, It is with great satisfaction that I recommend you to those artists and students who seek the truth in singing. Your understanding of the physiology of the vocal organs and your ability to produce the tones to demonstrate your teaching place your name amongst the world's greatest voice teachers.[15]

I may be wrong, but I suspect that the title of Professor had more to do with artistic promotion than any advanced academic qualifications. There are, incidentally, relations of Ward's still living locally and, without exception, those I spoke to referred to him as 'the Professor'.

Whatever his pedagogic status, he continued to teach throughout the 1930's and '40's, and also published three books: *The Keynote to Song and Good Health*, *The True Art of Bel Canto Singing*[16] and *Correct Breathing is Nature's Way to Perfect Health, Happiness and Success*. (The latter sounds like something that would sit perfectly in the Healthy Living section of bookshops today.) He was also a songwriter and, in 1949, published *Five Songs: An Album for Medium Voice*.

He may have retired from concert performances, but in the early 1940's he made several broadcasts on Radio Éireann, the precursor of RTE Radio One. On December 15, 1941, for instance, he performed a programme of songs by W. H Squire[17] and on May 9, 1942 and September 8, 1943, his repertoire featured songs by a wide variety of composers.[18] In 1949, he came to live in Dublin and the most recent reference I could find to his career as a teacher comes from the *Irish Independent* of August 26, 1950:

Professor Patrick Ward, International Singer and teacher of many famous singers, has vacancies for pupils. For terms and free brochure apply: Studios Messrs Gills, 15, Nassau Street, Dublin.

On March 13, 1965, in response to a reader's query in the *Evening Press*, 'Another Music Lover' wrote that Ward, 'a prophet without honour in his own land' was back living in London. I have often wondered why he retired from recording and performance at such a relatively young age, and then I came across a remarkable document; a typescript of an article by a Patrick Lacy who had met Ward in London 'just returned from Hollywood where he had been visited by hosts of celebrated screen stars'. I cannot vouch for the provenance or authenticity of this undated piece[19] (nor can the member of Ward's extended family who gave it to me) but the minute I saw its title – *Irish Caruso now a Yogi. He sees into the Future*[20] – I was, to put it mildly, intrigued.

The gist of the article is that Ward, 'at the height of his success as a concert and operatic artist, has forsaken fame and the footlights to devote himself to the study of the occult'. After meeting a 'distinguished Indian philosopher', he began to study 'the Art of Breathing as practised by followers of the Yoga creed, and found that by carrying out the lessons of his Indian teacher, he could banish all pain and make himself proof against every bodily ill'. There's more. He was 'able to see into the future' and 'predicted for one well-known actress a sudden burst of success that was realised the very next day'.

The upshot was that Ward, in a display of altruism that would have done Mother Teresa proud, 'decided to abandon his own artistic career in order to be able to place his services at the disposal of others'. Among those 'who clamoured for

Mr. Ward's advice and assistance' were Gracie Fields, Edward G. Robinson, Greta Garbo and Marlene Dietrich.

So far, I – and those I have spoken to – know very little about Patrick Ward's final years in London. I have been in contact with Jane D'Angelo, a fellow parishoner of Holy Apostles Church in Pimlico, who often visited Patrick and his wife Ann in their home. Patrick knew she was a soprano in the church choir so he showed her a copy of his song *Ave Maria* – written in 1946 – and asked her to sing it at his funeral. She promised she would.

Jane paints a poignant picture of the aftermath of Patrick's death on May 29, 1985: Ann refused to believe that her husband was dead and would not allow his body to be taken to the funeral directors. The priest asked Jane to keep her occupied until the body was removed. On the day of the funeral, mourners waited for Ann to arrive but, in the end, the mass had to start without her. Suddenly she appeared and walked up the aisle, approached the priest and said she was not staying because Patrick was not dead. She walked back out of the church and the funeral went ahead without her.

When Jane visited her later at her home in Sutherland Street, she said she was sorry Ann hadn't stayed for Patrick's mass and heard his *Ave Maria*. She asked her if she could play it. Ann sat at the piano and, as Jane sang for her, her eyes filled with tears.[21]

Mention Patrick Ward's name in Portlaoise today and, generally, it will mean nothing. Some people responded with 'Sure all the Wards were great singers',[22] but very few said any more than that. There were some vague memories: one man 'heard tell, years and years ago, about a Ward, only a young lad, who sang opera for a full hour standing on a wall in St. John's Square. You couldn't stir, the Square was so packed'.

In 2014, the late Maurice Kerry (1922-2015), recalled for me that, when he was six or seven, 'all the big shots of the town' went down to Limerick to hear Patrick Ward in concert. Maurice's father, Michael, was a friend of the Wards and when the singer came back to Portlaoise, he gave an impromptu recital outside Kerry's house on the New Road. 'He had a voice that could knock down the house', said Maurice, 'and the road outside was black with people'.

A voice that could knock down the house. What a great phrase. The publicity material for Ward's Parlophone records described him as Ireland's Greatest Ballad Singer; he himself always used the term 'Operatic tenor', while people I've played his music to, replaced 'operatic' with 'lyric' or 'light'. I seldom actually listen to tenors – or, for that matter, baritones, sopranos or contraltos – so I'll let others determine his technical merits. All I can say is that, whenever I hear Patrick Ward singing, my response is purely emotional and goes way beyond musical appreciation: I think of how he knew buildings I walk by every day; how he probably spoke to my ancestors who had shops on Main Street. I think of how he transcended humble origins, and I like to think that his father used to drink – and maybe sing – in my great-grandfather's pub just up the street from Lyster Lane.

Listen to Patrick Ward at
www.portlaoisepictures.com/patrickward.htm

NOTES

1. You can listen to music by more than one hundred local singers and musicians at www.portlaoisepictures.com
2. Griffith's Valuation of 1850 calls it Lester's Lane; the *Freeman's Journal* of July 13, 1886 has Leicester Lane, while the 1901 and 1911 censuses both have Lyster's Lane. Modern officialdom opts for Lyster Lane. Many years before the development of Lyster Square in the 1980's, the Lane, with houses both at right angles and parallel to the Main Street, was much more extensive than the short walk-

way it is today. In July 1886, Monsignor J. Phelan, Parish Priest of Maryborough, in a report to the Mountmellick Union, stated that 'out of 36 houses in Leicester Lane, only one was at all fit for human habitation'. They were not, he continued, 'even fit for dogs or horses'. It wasn't until 1936 that the inhabitants were finally moved out – many to the newly-built O'Moore Place – and the cottages eventually demolished.

3. Charles is buried in Boughlone graveyard, just off the Mountrath Road. His gravestone, 'erected by his sorrowing son Thomas', is one of only two clearly visible there.

4. *Laois Association Yearbook 1988*. Page 14. According to Mr. Meehan, Ward joined the Leinster Regiment, but in the *Irish Independent* of October 21, 1927, and other sources I've seen, he is described as an ex-Irish Guardsman.

5. Article on front page of *Bath & Wiltshire Chronicle & Herald*. June 15, 1950.

6. Marconi's mother was Annie Jameson of the famous Irish distillery family, so maybe he felt some affinity with her young compatriot.

7. September 14, 1985.

8. Larry Lustig, editor of *The Record Collector*.
    La Sheridan. Adorable Diva. Ann Chambers' biography of the opera star. Wolfhound Press, Dublin. 1989.

9. In March and April, 1964, The Beatles filmed numerous scenes from *A Hard Day's Night* here.

10. *Bath & Wiltshire Chronicle & Herald*. June 15, 1950.

11. Advertised in the *Saturday Herald*. June 26, 1926.

12. If you'd like to have a good laugh and, at the same time, sharpen your terpsichorean skills, have a listen to *Don't Sit On My Jimmy Shands* on the *Rumour and Sigh* album.

13. *Irish Independent*. February 3, 1931.

14. *Ibid*. February 9, 1932.

15. Letter to Patrick Ward from Maestro Molica. Naples. July, 1925.

16. According to its publicity material, 'the series of exercises in this book were practised by Caruso, Melba, Galli Curci, Tetrazzini, Chaliapin etc'.

17. British composer and Professor of cello at both the Royal College and Guildhall schools of music. In October, 1898, he was one of the earliest musicians to make a gramophone recording.

18. Details of Radio Éireann broadcasts courtesy Jack Smith, RTE Archives.

19. All I can deduce from the text is that it is pre-1953.

20. The aforementioned article by Patrick F. Meehan concludes by noting that Patrick Ward 'devoted his latter years to teaching Music and Palmistry'.

21. Neither Patrick nor Ann ever mentioned children to Jane, so I am

inclined to assume that they had none.

22. An exaggeration obviously, but one that contains a grain of truth. In the 1970's, Thomas 'Mario' Ward, a nephew of Patrick's, was a well-known singer in Galway, and various local Wards of my and others' acquaintance were, in Leonard Cohen's words, born with the gift of a golden voice. Young people I spoke to invariably mentioned Shayne Ward, winner of X Factor in 2005, who was born to Irish parents in Manchester.

ULYSSES IN LAOIS

Since it was first published in Paris in 1922, James Joyce's *Ulysses* continues to have a curious sort of dual existence. On one hand, it is regularly proclaimed the Greatest Modernist Novel: on the other, it is one of the Most Unfinished Masterpieces of World Literature; year after year, copies are bought with the best of intentions but, often as not, end up languishing in bookcases, unsold in charity shops, yellowing behind the sofa, even – and I have seen this – strategically positioned and forgotten about on expensive shelves and coffee tables. But seldom read from beginning to end.

On the simplest level, *Ulysses* concerns likeable Leopold Bloom, a canvasser of newspaper advertisements who, on the morning of Thursday, June 16, 1904, hasn't many reasons to be cheerful, and Stephen Dedalus whose intellectual posturing is the main reason so many readers say 'No' before they reach the book's final 'Yes'. Their comings and goings throughout Dublin city on that day are described in minute detail; they accidentally meet that night, enjoy a chat and a cup of cocoa, then go their separate ways. And that's the gist of it. Certainly not much in the line of what Joyce himself called a goahead plot.[1]

But this meagre skeleton is fleshed out with a vast corpus of scholarly apparatus, popular songs, arcane lore, uproarious comedy, Homeric parallels, allusions of all sorts, to say nothing of a plethora of styles, and a veritable host of characters, alive and dead, real and imaginary. Everything, in fact, bar the kitchen sink. No, I'm wrong. Said item does appear on page 591. Maybe Joyce wasn't entirely joking when he said that he'd put in enough enigmas and puzzles to keep the professors busy for centuries arguing over what he meant.[2]

But how does Laois – Queen's County as it was at the time of the book's composition – come into all this?

Very early on (60),[3] Mr. Bloom, on his way to buy a pork kidney for his breakfast, passes Saint Joseph's National School on Dorset Street and hears the children 'at their joggerfry'. His silent comment – 'Mine. Slieve Bloom.' – needs no explanation, but maybe the origin of the name (in Irish, *Sliabh Bladhma*) does. *Sliabh*, of course, means mountain, but there is no such certainty about *Bladhma*. One school of thought maintains that it refers to Bladh, a Milesian hero, while someone who knows the area like the back of his hand, tells us that the meaning of *Bladhma* is lost in the mists of time.[4] May I suggest that a more plausible translation is 'Mountain of Flame' (*Bladhma* is the genitive case of *Bladhm*, Irish for 'flame'), a reference to ancient Irish fire festivals such as *Samhain*, *Bealtaine*, and *Lughnasa* which were usually celebrated on high ground. I would also suggest that Joyce was familiar with the word *bladhm* because when the Slieve Blooms next appear – in the hilarious *Cyclops* chapter (341) – it is in the context of bonfires.

It is, in fact, *Cyclops* – where Joyce has a go at everything and anything from nationalism, racism and Yeatsian mysticism, to pet lovers, academic pomposity and the Bible – that has the greatest number of local allusions. In a parody of ancient Irish epics, we find Slieve Margy – the south-eastern corner of County Laois – whence, we are told, heroes voyaged to woo lovely maidens and, a few pages later (295), we meet Angus [*sic*] the Culdee, aka *Aengus Céile Dé* (Aengus, companion of God). This 8th century saint, like the more famous Fintan, is associated with the monastery of Clonenagh, the remains of which are still visible on the road between Portlaoise and Mountrath.

Then there's the virulently anti-English Citizen (modeled, most commentators believe, on Michael Cusack, one of the founders of the GAA) who curses 'the yellowjohns of Anglia' for trying 'to make us all die of consumption' by not draining 'millions of acres of marsh and bog' into the Barrow (which, of course, rises in the Slieve Blooms). A few lines later, he makes an impassioned plea: 'Save the trees of Ireland for the future men of Ireland on the fair hills of Eire, O'. To which, someone remarks that he has been reading 'a report of Lord Castletown's'. This is a reference to a House of Lords report on Irish Forestry[5] by the Rt. Honourable Bernard Edward Barnaby FitzPatrick, better known as Lord Castletown. Born in London in 1848, he was elected Conservative MP for Portarlington in 1880. A great supporter of the Gaelic League, he attended meetings dressed in a kilt and preferred to be addressed as *Mac Giolla Phádraig*. Somewhat surprising perhaps, given his friendship with King Edward VII? There are, incidentally, many references to that monarch in *Ulysses*, mostly scathing attacks on his Germanic ancestry, and his reputation as a warmonger and incorrigible Lothario: 'There's a bloody sight more pox than pax about that boyo. Edward Guelph Wettin!' (329).

Lord Castletown, who lived at Grantstown Manor, Ballacolla, was also president of the Wild Birds Protection Society, and noted that there were no less than eighty-two species of birds in the Queen's County. His last major public appearance was in Maryborough in November, 1928 at the unveiling of the memorial to soldiers who lost their lives in World War I. After Lord Castletown's death, Grantstown

Manor was sold out of the Fitzpatrick family and in 1947 much of it was destroyed by fire.

In the carriage to a friend's funeral in Glasnevin Cemetery (97), Mr. Bloom passes the Rotunda Maternity Hospital which, later on, in the *Sirens* episode, Blazes Boylan also passes en route to his assignation with Bloom's wife, Molly. The Rotunda was founded by Bartholomew Mosse who was born in Maryborough in 1712. He became a surgeon specializing in midwifery and in 1745 opened a small hospital in George's Lane (now South Great George's Street), Dublin. This Hospital for Poor Lying-in Women was the first maternity hospital in the British Isles. In 1757, a much larger one – the New Lying-In Hospital, with Mosse as its Master – opened on the present site in Parnell Square. (It was renamed the Rotunda following the construction of an adjoining round entertainment room used to raise funds for the hospital).

Bartholomew Mosse died destitute[6] in 1759 and was buried in an unmarked grave in Donnybrook Cemetery. His last resting place was eventually identified, and in 1995 a memorial stone was erected nearby. The following year, a plaque was erected by Laois Heritage Society on his birthplace, Annefield House, Dublin Road, Portlaoise. He remains one of only two Maryborough people honoured on an Irish postage stamp. The other is the aviator Colonel James Fitzmaurice (1898-1965) of whom there is, of course, no sign in the crowded skies of *Ulysses*.

A quick jump from airplanes to motor cars. In 1900, the Gordon Bennett Cup, an annual international road race, was instituted by the American sportsman and owner of the *New York Herald*, James Gordon Bennett. On account of England winning it the previous year, the 1903 race should have been run there (a bit like Eurovision!), but because there was now a speed limit of 12 mph on all English roads, a town-to-town race was impossible, so it was moved to a closed circuit through Kildare, Queen's County and Carlow. The race was won for Germany by Camille Jenatzy whose red beard and furious driving – his average speed was 49.2 mph – earned him the nickname *Le Diable Rouge*. Ten years after his success, the Red Devil came to an undignified end. As a joke during a hunting party on his estate, he hid in the bushes and started grunting like a wild boar. One of his companions promptly shot him dead. Joyce drew on the 1903 race for a short story[7] and there are three references in *Ulysses*. The first during small talk at the funeral in Glasnevin (99), the second in a joke involving bolting horses and a corpse (100), and the third in Bella Cohen's whorehouse (491). And, finally, our unfortunate porcine impersonator himself is the subject of a drunken prediction (424).

On its way to Glasnevin, the cortege crosses the Royal Canal (101) where Bloom sees a barge full of 'turf from the midland bogs'. The same barge appears later (221) where it inspires Rev. John Conmee S.J. to reflect on 'the providence of the Creator', and in an episode set in Holles Street Maternity Hospital – where Joyce makes the English language jump through all sorts of linguistic hoops in imitation of the nine months of development from conception to birth – the bargeman, à la the diarist Samuel Pepys, bears news of a drought in the Midlands (393).

On page 240, a character reminds himself to borrow 'those reminiscences of sir Jonah Barrington' from a friend of his. Born at Knapton, near Abbeyleix in 1760, Barrington was a judge and historian whose extravagance led to dubious financial practices; so dubious, in fact, that, in 1830, he was removed from judicial office.[8] He left Ireland never to return and died in Versailles in 1834. Today he is best remembered for his *Personal Sketches of His Own Times* which gives a lively and sometimes grotesque account – Chapter XXII, for instance, features cannibalism and a priest bisected by a portcullis – of his tumultuous life and times.

The next Laoisman we encounter just a few pages later is Joseph Hutchinson, Lord Mayor of Dublin from 1904 to 1906.[9] He was born in Borris-in-Ossory in 1852 and, at the age of fifteen, went to live in Dublin. In 1890, he entered politics and was elected Councillor for Dublin Corporation. He devoted himself to gaining non-contributory pensions for Corporation workmen, and when such a Bill was eventually passed in the House of Commons, Dublin was the first city in the Empire to enjoy such a privilege. In 1896, he was appointed High Sheriff for that year and, in 1904, elected Lord Mayor. On page 246, in a discussion on Dublin politics, the assistant town clerk complains about the lack of organisation at meetings of Dublin Corporation: 'Where was the marshal, he wanted to know, to keep order in the council chamber... no mace on the table, nothing in order, no quorum even and Hutchinson the lord mayor in Llandudno...' On October, 17, 1928, Joseph Hutchinson's wife died. He himself died the next day.

The marshal mentioned above was City Marshall, John Howard Parnell (older brother of Charles Stewart) and there are several references to the family scattered throughout the text, most memorably perhaps when Bloom ponders the eccentric ways of the Parnell siblings (164-165). The family originated in Cheshire whence, in 1660, Thomas Parnell, a staunch supporter of Cromwell, fearing the restoration of the monarchy, came to Ireland. He settled in Rathleague, just outside Maryborough, and subsequent generations resided there until the 1830's, after which time the house fell into disrepair. Part of the original building was incorporated into Rathleague House, a private residence today.

From politics to poetry. On page 545, in a paragraph about missing persons, we are asked 'does anybody hereabouts remember Caoc O'Leary, a favourite and most trying declamation piece, by the way, of poor John Casey and a bit of perfect poetry in its own small way?' The poem referred to is *Caoch the Piper* and in it, the eponymous Caoch O'Leary goes away and isn't seen again for twenty years. It was, in fact, written by John Keegan[10] who was born in the townland of Killeaney near Shanahoe in 1816. His literary career began in 1837 when the *Leinster Express* published *The Rifleman's Grave* and he subsequently contributed stories and poems to a wide variety of magazines. He also became part of *The Nation* group of poets which included Thomas Davis, author of the still-popular *A Nation Once Again* and *The West's Asleep*. Keegan died of cholera in Dublin in 1849 and is buried in Glasnevin Cemetery.

Keegan's writings were of great interest to John Canon O'Hanlon,[11] that eminent Laoisman whose own work[12] is invaluable to anyone with the slightest interest in the history of our county. Born in Stradbally in 1821, his family emigrated to Missouri where he studied for the priesthood. Following his ordination, he worked in various parishes until ill-health brought him back to Ireland. On his recovery, he served in different capacities in the archdiocese of Dublin and, in 1880, was appointed parish priest of Sandymount. It is here that we find the *Ulysses* connection. Near twilight on the evening of June 16, Bloom, on his way from visiting the bereaved Dignam family, stops for a rest on Sandymount Strand.

But there is more to his relaxation than meets the eye: he is, in fact, surreptitiously ogling young Gerty MacDowell who is minding children on the strand. And Gerty is no shrinking violet: she is well aware that Bloom is 'eyeing her as a snake eyes its prey' (358) and, as the sexual tension rises, Joyce flits between it and descriptions of Benediction in the nearby Star of the Sea church. It is here that Canon O'Hanlon's presence pervades the pages like incense. Joyce's mingling of sanctity and sex will not be to everyone's liking, but it is certainly neither prurient nor gratuitous. On the contrary, he – a writer never noted for his love of the clergy – portrays the Canon in a very sympathetic light. Gerty, for instance, recalls how understanding he was in the confession box (Surely a trait that differentiated him from many of his clerical colleagues at the turn of the twentieth century?) and that 'he looked almost like a saint… he was so kind and holy' (356). We catch our last glimpse of the Canon, resplendent in 'cloth of gold cope' much later in a night-marish sequence (450) where his mantelpiece clock plays a leading role in mocking poor Bloom's cuckoldry.

In the vast, secular catechism that is the *Ithaca* episode, Bloom recalls that in 1885 he had 'publicly expressed his adherence to the collective and national economic programme advocated by James Fintan Lalor' (637). Born in Tinakill, Raheen, in 1807, Lalor's education was limited by protracted ill-health. Despite his perceived disabilities,[13] he joined Young Ireland, the nationalist movement founded by a group of young radicals associated with *The Nation* newspaper, and became a staunch advocate of agrarian reform.

In 1847, he contributed a series of letters to *The Nation*, demanding the land of Ireland for the people of Ireland. Despite the failure of the Young Ireland rebellion of 1848, Lalor, in an attempt to ignite another rising, led an attack on the Royal Irish Constabulary barracks in Cappoquin. He was arrested and died of bronchitis in prison in December, 1849. It is said that his funeral attracted 25,000 mourners.[14] Finally, I'll just mention that the Fintan Lalor Pipe Band from Dublin makes a fleeting appearance in *Finnegans Wake*,[15] the book that Joyce himself said was intended for the 'ideal reader suffering from an ideal insomnia'.[16]

Also in *Ithaca* (579), there's a reference to Lord Antony MacDonnell, Irish Under-Secretary from 1902 to 1908. He was known as 'The Bengal Tiger' from his time as Governor of that region, but it is his brother, Mark Anthony Mac Donnell, who is of most interest here. When no local anti-Parnellite candidate could be found to contest the General Election of 1892 in the Leix Division of Queen's County, Dr. McDonnell, a native of Mayo working as a surgeon in the Liverpool Cancer and Skin Hospital, was, to use a modern idiom, parachuted in. He won the seat and, in 1895 and 1900, was returned unopposed. In January 1906 he resigned and, six months later, in a cruel twist of fate, died of cancer.[17]

But let's return to Mr. Bloom. Earlier, in the *Freeman's Journal* offices (120), he daydreams about the power of his own profession, how it is advertisements that sell newspapers, not boring, official jargon like 'Demesne situate in the townland of Rosenallis, the barony of Tinnahinch'. Situated in north County Laois, in the foothills of the Slieve Bloom mountains, Rosenallis is noted for its Society of Friends (Quaker) graveyard just outside the village. William Edmundson, the ex-soldier who brought Quakerism to Ireland, lies buried there. In this episode too (136), a report on a 'great Nationalist meeting' in Borris-in-Ossory is mocked by Myles Crawford, the newspaper's editor: 'All balls! Bulldosing the public! Give them something with a bite in it. Put us all into it, damn its soul. Father Son and Holy Ghost and Jakes McCarthy'.

As talk in the office turns to the notorious Phoenix Park murders of May 6, 1882, someone mentions Skin-the-Goat 'who drove the car'. There are numerous references to the murders in *Ulysses* (83, 137, 542, 549, 562) and this particular one is to James Fitzharris, a cabman convicted of aiding and abetting the assassins. The local connection is that Fitzharris – whose nickname, incidentally, came from the story that during hard times he killed his goat and sold the skin – spent sixteen years in Maryborough Jail.

At one stage, Crawford proclaims that the eminent statesman and orator Henry Grattan once wrote for his paper (the oldest in Ireland, incidentally, when it merged with the *Irish Independent* in 1924). The Grattans had an ancestral link to our county and, in 1782, Henry acquired the Moyanna estate near Vicarstown where he built a shooting lodge at Dunrally. An aqueduct carrying the Grand Canal over the Derryvarragh River is named after him, and Dunrally Bridge over the Barrow was built by his son James in 1820. James, incidentally, contributed £4,000 towards the building of the old County Infirmary in Maryborough. Over the years, this fine edifice on the Dublin road has seen many changes; hospital, County Council offices, neglected disgrace, and eventual refurbishment in 2005 as the Grattan Business Centre.

The Grattan family had considerable influence on the development of Vicarstown. Henry's granddaughter Pauline Grattan Bellew provided the site and financial assistance for the Church of the Assumption and, in 1868, built the village National School. In 1882, she built Grattan Lodge on the site where Henry had planted beech trees shortly after acquiring his estate. He had, apparently, a great love for trees and the story goes that when a visitor to his home at Tinnahinch, Co. Wicklow, remarked that one was dangerously close to the house, he replied 'Yes, I have often thought of moving the house'.

In 1820, en route to Parliament, too ill to bear the jolting of a carriage, Henry Grattan travelled by canal from Liverpool to London where he died on June 4. There is a certain irony in this final journey: when the Grand Canal was being built in Vicarstown (1789-91), he allowed it to go through his estate free of charge. For reasons apparently lost in the mists of time, his wish to be buried in Moyanna was disregarded and he was laid to rest in Westminster Abbey instead. But his memory is still alive in many parts of Ireland. The family coat of arms, for instance, is still visible on the archway leading into Moyanna graveyard and there is a Grattan Street in Portlaoise and other Irish towns. *Ulysses* refers to both Grattan Bridge at Capel Street (252) and the 'stern stone hand' of his statue on College Green (228). We take our leave of Henry himself on page 526, where, in a surreal parody of an ancient Greek myth, he springs up from the earth to engage in mortal combat with Wolfe Tone.

And now we arrive at Maryborough railway station, the last stop on our Joycean tour of Laois. Since it opened in 1847,[18] the station has seen all sorts of comings and goings, and one of them found its way from Joyce's imagination into the pages of *Ulysses*. In the long gush of unpunctuated interior monologue that concludes the book, Molly is lying in bed thinking of this, that, and the other; her girlhood in Gibraltar, her lovers, the death of her young son, bits of songs and novels, the ups-and-downs of marriage, her dalliance with Blazes Boylan... This episode has inspired music, plays, films, and God knows how many lofty dissertations but, for my purposes here, all I'm interested in is where Molly – as usual, pondering her husband's imperfections – recalls an incident at the station (669):

> ...something always happens with him the time going to the Mallow concert at Maryborough ordering boiling soup for the two of us then the bell rang out he walks down the platform with the soup splashing about taking spoonfuls of it hadnt he the nerve and the waiter after him making a holy show of us screeching and confusion for the engine to start but he wouldnt pay till he finished it the two gentlemen in the 3rd class carriage said he was

quite right so he was too hes so pigheaded sometimes when he gets a thing into his head a good job he was able to open the carriage door with his knife or theyd have taken us on to Cork…

On that note, let us take our leave of Mr. Joyce and all the Dubliners and Laoisites – there's a word that might have satisfied the punster and scatologist in him – that populate the pages of this masterpiece, his usylessly unreadable Blue Book of Eccles.[19]

NOTES

1. In a letter to one of his patrons, Harriet Weaver, December 21, 1926.
2. *James Joyce* by Richard Ellmann. 1977 edition, p. 535.
3. There are so many editions of Joyce's work available now that it would be impossible to refer to them all. Page numbers in this essay refer to the Penguin paperback edition first published in 1968 and reprinted many times since.
4. In his Introduction to *Bladhma*. Thomas P. Joyce in association with the *Leinster Express*. 1995.
5. The reference is, in fact, anachronistic as the report was not presented until 1908.
6. *Dublin 1745-1922: Hospitals, Spectacle & Vice*. Gary A. Boyd. Four Courts Press. Dublin, 2006.
7. *After the Race* in *Dubliners*.
8. *A Dictionary of Irish Biography*. Henry Boylan. Gill & Macmillan, Dublin 1978.
9. For much of my information on James Hutchinson, I am indebted to the late Patrick F. Meehan for an interesting piece in the *Laois Association Yearbook 1989*.
10. For more information see *John Keegan, Selected Works*. Edited by Tony Delaney. Galmoy Press 1997. Joyce is confusing John Keegan with the Fenian poet John Keegan Casey (1846-1870) who, under the pen name 'Leo', also contributed to *The Nation* and wrote the words of the well-known song *The Rising of the Moon*.
11. *Legends and Poems. John Keegan*. Collected and edited by Very Rev. John Canon O'Hanlon. Dublin, 1907.
12. Especially *History of the Queen's County*. Volume I by V. Rev. John Canon O'Hanlon and Rev. Edward O'Leary, was originally published in 1907. Volume II, compiled chiefly from the papers of

the late Canon O'Hanlon by Rev. Edward O'Leary and Rev. Matthew Lalor, appeared in 1914. Both were reprinted by Roberts Books, Kilkenny, 1981. For more information see *John Canon O'Hanlon, the man and his legacy*. Teddy Fennelly. Arderin Publishing, Portlaoise, 2005.

13. According to Henry Boylan's *A Dictionary of Irish Biography*, Lalor was 'near-sighted, deaf and ungainly'.

14. In December, 1949, the local James McIntosh Cumann of Fianna Fáil proposed to the Town Commission that Coote Street be renamed Lalor Street (or James Fintan Lalor Street, depending on which local newspaper you read). This, of course, never happened. On December 15, 2007, a statue of Lalor was officially unveiled in the grounds of County Hall, Portlaoise by then Tánaiste Brian Cowen and, in September, 2013, the inaugural JFL School was held in the town.

15. *Finnegans Wake*. Page 25. Faber paperback. 1975.

16. *Ibid*. p. 120.

17. *The Members of Parliament for Laois & Offaly (Queen's and King's Counties) 1801-1918* by Patrick F. Meehan. Published by the Leinster Express (1972) Ltd. in 1983. Pages 62-63.

18. After an experimental run in April witnessed by 'crowds of the peasantry cheering and waving their hats as the train passed', the station was opened on June 26, 1847. These events were widely reported in local and national papers of the time.

19. Joyce's own ironic estimation of the book in *Finnegans Wake* (p. 179). The first edition of *Ulysses* had a blue cover. The Blooms lived in Eccles Street.

OUR WAR MEMORIAL

...and the blood of children ran through the streets without fuss,
like children's blood.
Pablo Neruda (1904-1973)

World War I was declared on July 28, 1914 and lasted until November 11, 1918. It is estimated that nine million soldiers and about seven million innocent civilians were killed. At least twenty million people were wounded. St. Peter's Church in the Market Square holds a copy of the eight volumes of Ireland's Memorial Records (1923) which contain the names and details of 49,647 Irishmen who died in the war.

Under overcast skies on Thursday, November 15, 1928, more than 500 people, including almost 200 ex-soldiers and relatives of the fallen, gathered in Bank Place/Church Street for the official unveiling of the town's War Memorial, erected by their surviving comrades to honour the memory of the 177 Officers and men of the 4th Battalion, the Leinster Regiment (Royal Queen's County's Regiment) who died in the conflict.[1] Almost a century later, it is still very moving to read the familiar names: to think that many of these brave men once walked our streets, spoke with our accents, cheered for local teams.

None of my direct ancestors were killed in the war, yet

whenever I see the names of the three Dunnes inscribed there, I sometimes shiver, even in the brightest sunlight. I can only imagine the emotion our forebears felt as they gathered at the monument in 1928: what memories filled their bowed heads when, at midday, they observed two minutes silence.

Major W. D. Hamilton, one of the surviving officers and Chairman of the Organising Committee, opened proceedings and then invited Lord Castletown of Upper Ossory,[2] former Commander of the regiment, to perform the unveiling. In his address, Lord Castletown outlined the history of the 4th battalion which, following the creation of the Irish Free State, had been disbanded in 1922. The latter act he condemned as one 'of deep obloquy'. He also referred to the recent Armistice Day ceremonies when 'every town, village and house was scarlet with poppies' and concluded by mentioning the 'ghastly ordeal' of war, and the communal sorrow for 'those who were with us but have gone and left us'. Then, amid great applause, he unveiled the Memorial.

Monsignor Michael J. Murphy – former Professor of Theology at Carlow College, Parish Priest of Maryborough for forty years from 1901, and chaplain to the 4th Leinster Regiment until it was disbanded – blessed the Memorial, and the ceremony ended with The Last Post and a funeral march played by the British Legion Band.

A small decorative bowl and fountain once adorned the Memorial. I can never recall seeing it in working order, but I do remember it full of ice in winter and stagnant water in the summertime, with just one of the two small cups still attached. The structure still features a maple leaf design; a reference to the fact that one of the battalions of the Leinsters had its origins in Canada. Following British Army reforms in 1881, the battalion moved to Ireland where the Leinster Regiment's depot was established at Crinkill Barracks, near Birr.

As might be expected, the monument caused some controversy in the locality. When members of the regiment initially sought to honour their fallen comrades, the Finance Committee of the County Council recommended that a site should not be granted. The issue became something of a political football until, following a full meeting of the Council in 1926, permission was granted by 13 votes to 7. And so the Memorial – designed by architect Thomas Scully and built by Thomas Hearne & Son (all from Waterford) – went ahead. But that wasn't the end of it. The cement was hardly dry when a pseudonymous writer to *The Irish Times* (November 22, 1928) wondered why it was 'made of Carlow limestone when the Queen's County limestone is the nicest of all?'

In 1990, after a lapse of many years, an Armistice Commemoration was revived at the Memorial and is now an annual event, attended by civic, religious and military figures, townspeople and, most fittingly of all, descendents of those who died in the war. In 2001, the County Council decided to relocate the Memorial and so, stone by stone, it was dismantled and rebuilt in what is now officially known as the Memorial Park in Millview. At the time, there was considerable local unease, with some believing that the move was simply to facilitate commercial development in the Church Street area but, personally, I feel that the council got it exactly right, and the new location is much more conducive to reflection and remembrance of why the Memorial exists in the first place.

Around that time too, a panel commemorating United Nations troops was added to the Memorial, something which I think has compromised its aesthetic integrity. Since 2008 however, the Memorial Park also features a separate and beautiful memorial to those who served with the United Nations and the effect is one of enhancing what I think is potentially[3] one of the town's loveliest civic areas.

Φ

The Great War has inspired countless artistic endeavours in all disciplines and I will conclude by recommending two which mean a lot to me. I feel proud that one of the very best WWI novels I've read is by New York-based Mountmellick man, Tom Phelan. Moving from the tranquillity of the Irish Midlands to the horrors of Passchendaele and Ypres, *The Canal Bridge* paints an unforgettable picture of what men and animals endured. The song *Never Any Good* by the English musician and songwriter Martin Simpson is only indirectly connected with the war, but I can never listen to its depiction of a wonderful, infuriating, affectionate, flawed Everyman and remain unmoved.

NOTES

1. Short biographical details by Patrick Hogarty of some of the soldiers commemorated on the Monument (as the War Memorial is usually called by townspeople) were published in the Laois Heritage Society Journal, Volume 2, 2004. Also, the National Archives of Ireland hold more than 9,000 wills of enlisted Irish soldiers. Each comprising no more than a few handwritten lines, they are heartbreaking to read. They can be searched online at http://soldierswills.nationalarchives.ie/search/sw/home.jsp

2. Born Bernard Edward Barnaby FitzPatrick, His Lordship was, *inter alia*, Conservative MP for Portarlington in the 1880's and Chancellor of the Royal University of Ireland from 1906 to 1910. In his leisure time, he was a keen ornithologist, a writer and cultural enthusiast (surprisingly perhaps, a staunch supporter of the Irish language) and the story goes that he kept a 14ft python in his rooms until it attacked and almost killed a chambermaid. Upon his death without issue at Grantstown Manor in 1937, the title Lord Castletown was discontinued. In 1965, his extensive archive was presented to the National Library of Ireland by his nephew.

3. More regular attention needs to be paid to its maintenance; on more than one occasion I've seen the site covered with almost as many dandelions as blades of grass.

THE ELECTRIC CINEMA

In the 1820's, members of the Delany family from Clonad moved into Maryborough where they became engaged in the tailoring business. They lived on the Main Street, opposite Bull Lane. Griffith's Valuation records an Alicia Delany living there in the 1850's and, in Slater's *Directory of Ireland* (1870), we find tailors Daniel and Martin Delany. The latter is also listed in Main Street in the 1881 edition. The family eventually moved to the Lower Square where, according to the Census return for that year, Martin Delany and his wife Julia were living in 1901.[1]

Martin was succeeded by his son Paul, a master tailor, who had learned his craft in his uncle John's establishment in Chester. An advertisement in the *Leinster Express* from 1905 proudly proclaimed 'the latest fashions, the newest materials, the best workmanship. Established over 75 years'. Paul and his sister Mary appear in the 1911 Census as draper and tailor's cutter, and draper's assistant respectively, but the entry gives us little idea of the extent of their business; as well as its thriving general drapery, a team of journeyman tailors made bespoke garments in a workshop at the rear of the shop. But Paul obviously had other interests as well...

The first dedicated cinema in Ireland, the Volta on Dublin's Mary Street, opened its doors in 1909. Its unlikely manager was none other than James Joyce/Signor Giacomo

Joyce, home for a while from his self-imposed exile in Trieste. Neither Joyce nor his Italian partners (one of whom was described by Joyce's father as 'the hairy mechanic with the lion tamer's coat') had any cinematic experience and, given that most of the pictures shown were in Italian (with pamphlets distributed to explain what was happening), their audience turned out to be mostly poor people seeking warmth and shelter. It's hardly surprising that the venture lasted less than a year…

Five years later, Paul Delany opened the Maryborough Electric Cinema on the Well/New Road. In one week in August, 1915, for instance, you had a choice of three feature films, plus a variety of shorts and 'the latest news in pictures'. Live music was by Bannan's Orchestra and tickets cost 1/6 (one shilling and sixpence) and 'a very limited number at 3d (three pence)'. One of my oldest interviewees recalled how, during the Silent Era, John Lynch used to 'patrol the gods with a big stick' and woe betide those who, today, we would call 'messers'. He also remembered the comments hurled at the musicians if what they were playing wasn't music to their ears!

In 1919, Paul Delany married May Webb of the famous Dublin bookshop family[2] and they moved to the recently-built Kellyville Park where family members still reside today. In February, 1928, Paul Delany placed an ad in *The Irish Times* seeking tenders for building a new cinema and, in 1932, the town had the new Electric Cinema on the site of the old. Over the years, it was not uncommon to see groups of people gazing into the window of Paul Delany's drapery shop on the Lower Square. I'm sure they were admiring the latest fashions as well, but the main attraction were the cinema listings posted there each week.

In May, 1933, the cinema showed *Sweet Inniscarra*, one of the first 'talkies' made in Ireland. Shot in Cashel and

Portarlington, it featured members of the latter town's Dramatic Class with a musical score by the No. 1 Free State Army Band.[3] I'm sure that was a quieter occasion than the night in the 1940's when fire broke out in the cinema. As recounted to me by the late Paul Delany Jnr, it started during the screening of a film starring future US president Ronald Reagan but, thankfully, the only casualties were 'fourteen or fifteen reels burnt to a cinder'.

After Paul Delany's death in 1953, both the drapery and cinema were continued by his sons Paul Jnr, John, and daughter Sheila. By day, Edward 'Ned' Farrell' from Church Street was a mechanic in Aldritt's engineering works on Tower Hill; by night, often assisted by his namesake Joe, he was the projectionist in the Electric cinema. I can still hear the ironic cheers whenever the projector broke down, but when it came to keeping order in 'the pit', Jack Pierce's torch was as lethal as any six-gun on the screen. ('Quiet there or ye'll go out!' And, on one mortifying occasion, 'Quiet there young Dunne or I'll tell your father!)

I saw scores of films in *Paul's*, but one, above all others, has colonised my memory. Years ago – in a perfect example of having too much time on my hands – I read a lengthy exegesis of several James Bond films. Among other revelations, I learned that Ursula Andress emerging from the sea in *Dr. No* is an allusion to Aphrodite rising from the waves. After seeing that film in 1963, I can tell you that, for nights afterwards, it wasn't Greek mythology I was dreaming of.

In 1968, *Helga* – no, not the ship involved in the 1916 Rising – caused a bit of a stir in the town. I never saw what was widely derided as soft porn disguised as sex education but, recently, I did see a trailer online: asked her opinion of the contraceptive pill, a young woman working in a cocktail bar utters the immortal words: 'the greatest thing since popcorn'. Over the years, the lads I've spoken to who did see 'the complete intimate story of a young girl with its scenes never before shown', outnumber those who claim to have been in the GPO in 1916.

In 1968, the Delany family sold the cinema to a local consortium (Seán Keenan from Mountmellick; Peter Dunne, Seán Ryan and Harry Dempsey from Portarlington). It was completely refurbished and Timmy Scully became the new manager. But in the following year, the Electric Cinema closed for good and an important part of the town's social and cultural history was, so to speak, gone with the wind. The building subsequently housed International Screenprint and a Chinese Restaurant.

NOTES

1. For more information on the Delany family, see 'The Delany Family' in *Portlaoise Photo Lore* by Johnny O'Brien. Arderin Publishing Co., Portlaoise. 2001

2. Poet and novelist Padraic Colum (1881-1972) – who wrote most of the words of the popular song *She Moved Through the Fair* – called George Webb 'that most knowing of all booksellers'. His shop on Dublin's Aston Quay also gets a mention in James Joyce's story *The Dead*.

3. The film received decidedly mixed reviews: one critic complained that the production and acting were on 'the lowest amateur level', that the story was 'padded out with scenes and songs which have nothing to do with the action.' (*The Kinematograph Weekly* February 22, 1934). On the other hand, according to an article in the *Laois Association Yearbook 1996-97*, the man from the *Daily Express* rhapsodised that, because of the film, '1933 will be a more important date in Irish history'.

OUR RUSSIAN TROPHY

Until it was annexed by Russia and exploded on to global headlines in March, 2014, the Crimea, on the northern shores of the Black Sea, was for most people the stuff of distant schooldays memories; moral tales of Florence Nightingale, 'The Lady with the Lamp', or the galloping rhythm of *The Charge of the Light Brigade*:

> Half a league, half a league
> Half a league onward
> All in the valley of Death
> Rode the six hundred

Many songs, stories and poems were inspired by actual events in the Crimean War (1853-1856), the convoluted causes of which lie outside the scope of this article: suffice to say that the conflict centred around battles at the Alma, Balaclava, Inkerman and, most prominently, the attempt by allies Britain, France and Turkey to destroy the Russian Black Sea fleet in the naval base of Sevastopol.

After a winter-long siege, and many non-combat deaths from cold, hunger and disease, the allies eventually captured Sevastopol. As proof of its victory over the Russians – and also to act as ballast – hundreds of cannon were brought back by the British Army and distributed throughout the Empire. This article describes how one of them found its way to Maryborough, seventeen hundred miles to the west, and what happened to it thereafter.

On October 8, 1857, the Town Commissioners applied to the Secretary of State for War for 'a trophy of some description' which, 'placed in a conspicuous part of our town, would act as a stimulus to many to join the ranks of the British Army and fight in the battles of the country, as their friends and relatives have heretofore done'.[1] Their request met with a positive response from Lord Panmure, and the 'loyal inhabitants of Maryborough' were duly presented with a cannon captured at Sevastopol.[2] He announced that the gun, 'suggestive of such reminiscences of the endurance and valour of the warriors of Great Britain and Ireland must become an object of pride and attraction'.[3]

The original plan was to erect a portico at the courthouse, on top of which the gun would be mounted. I don't know how, but it ended up, not at the courthouse, but on a stone pedestal in the Market Square or, as it was officially known at the time, Market Place. On June 9, 1858, the foundation stone of the pedestal was laid by Mr. John McEvoy, hotelier and Chairman of the Town Commission. That evening, there was a celebratory dinner, to which the *Leinster Express* of June 12, referred with uncharacteristic levity: 'Among others, our reporter received a card but he, hapless poor wight, was unable to attend. The toothache had previous possession and we can well have imagined him apostrophising the enemy as Burns did heretofore:

My curse upon your venom'd stang
That shoots my tortur'd gums alang.'

On Tuesday, July 27, the people of Maryborough

assembled *en masse* to celebrate the installation of the gun – transported from the Royal Arsenal in Woolwich – and its presentation to Dr. Thomas Pilsworth,[4] the newly-elected Chairman of the Town Commission. His Vice-Chairman was solicitor Thomas Turpin who later described the event as the proudest day of his life. He was also, apparently, a man unburdened by modesty: 'I assume to myself the credit of being the instigator or promoter of gaining that trophy...'[5]

The Secretary for War was represented by Colonel Francis Plunkett Dunne and the Queen's County Royal Rifles. Also present for the occasion, which featured fulsome speeches, flags, patriotic music and 'such cheers as were never before heard in Maryborough', were many of 'the leading gentlemen' of the county, Town Commissioners distinguished by their pink rosettes, and ladies spectating from their carriages. And let us not forget artilleryman Hovenden who had lost a leg at Sevastopol, and now, 'decorated with several medals, sat at the breech of the gun, waving the Union Jack with evident pride'. Such was his enthusiasm that he managed to mount the cannon, and call for three cheers for the Queen which were met with 'a thrilling response'.[6]

The patriotic Hovenden and the 'half a dozen stalwart fellows with Crimean medals on their breasts who gathered round the trophy their valour had helped to secure' were just a handful of an estimated 30,000 Irish soldiers who fought in the Crimea.[7] Further research may reveal more local names but, as of today, I can only identify two veterans from Maryborough, both of whom, I was intrigued to learn, once lived in Market Place...

I'm not sure of how and when the Templings, a British Army family, first came to Maryborough, but it is possible that Private James Templing of the 21st Regiment of Foot met his future wife during his tour of duty in Stradbally and Maryborough (and other Irish towns) between 1827 and

1831. They had two sons, Joseph and James, the former born in Weedon, Northamptonshire, in 1834; the latter in the East Indies c. 1842. (Both locations were where their father was stationed at the time.) Joseph followed his father into the same regiment and spent more than twenty-two years in the army, serving in Malta, East Indies, West Indies and the Crimea. During the latter campaign he was awarded the Crimean War medal with Clasp for Sebastopol [sic] and the Turkish War Medal. He was also decorated for long service and good conduct. Joseph left the army in 1877 and retired to Maryborough where he lived at No. 5, Market Place and earned his living as a whitesmith. In my mind's eye I see him on summer evenings, standing in his doorway, gazing at the cannon, and I wonder what memories are occupying his mind. Comradeship and bravery? Anguish and blood? Or is he marvelling at how, after all his years of soldiering, he survived without the slightest injury or wound?[8]

I also imagine Mrs. Frances Grennan watching the celebrations of July 27 from her upstairs window at No. 11, Market Place. And I wonder what is going through her mind. Is she cursing all wars, or proudly thinking of her son Edward[9], one of Tennyson's 'six hundred' at Balaclava. In 1861, after eleven years in the army, he was discharged, deemed medically unfit for further service because of varicose veins. On his discharge papers, his intended place of residence was given as Market Place, Maryborough but, in 1862, he went to Australia where he lived the rest of his life. Sadly, he ended his days in the hospital ward of Melbourne Immigrants' Home, 'friendless and paralysed, indebted to strangers for a roof over his head and a crust to eat'.[10] The inscription on his headstone in Melbourne General Cemetery reads:

To One Of The Noble Six Hundred
In memory of Edward Grennan, native of
Queen's Co. Ireland who, as a soldier of the
4th Light Dragoons, fought at Alma, Inkerman
and Sebastopol and also with the Light
Brigade at Balaclava. He died at Royal Park,
Melbourne, 14th December 1896, aged 61
years. May God have mercy on his soul.

A number of fictional Queen's County men also
featured in the Crimea *via* the pages of *The Connaught
Rangers, A Tale of the Crimean War*, a short story by Nenagh-
born John Augustus O'Shea published in 1884.[11] Set on St.
Patrick's Day, 1855, and rendered in what today reads like
awful stage Irishry ('Musha, 'tis aisy cry hault…'), the story
includes two characters from our county: one, an unnamed
soldier educated 'in the Christian Brothers at Maryboro' who
once served in the Queen's County Royal Rifles; the other, a
Dr. Le Blanc – 'the heart's blood of a daycent fellow' – from
Portarlington.

But back to the real world. In his address, Colonel
Dunne hoped 'there would never be an occasion to disturb
the cannon from its pedestal; that it would always remain in
the safe and loyal keeping of the Town Commissioners and
the inhabitants of Maryborough'.[12] But such an occasion did
indeed come to pass. Before we come to that, a quick mention
of the celebrations that continued with a sumptuous dinner at
which there were more speeches, numerous toasts 'drunk
with acclamation', and music by the band of the Queen's
County Royal Rifles whose repertoire ranged from old
reliables like *Auld Lang Syne* and *The British Grenadiers* to the
intriguing *Queen's County Quickstep*.

But let's leave the gentlemen to their brandy and
cigars, and skip forward more than twenty years. The Town

Commissioners in 1880 were clearly of a different political persuasion to their 1858 predecessors because they wrote to Major-General J. R. Glyn, CB, Commander of the Dublin District (which included Queen's County), requesting the removal from the Market Square [sic] of what they now considered an 'obstruction and a nuisance'. In his fairly barbed reply, Major-General Glyn stated that, provided the expense was borne by the local authority, he would be prepared to remove the gun to 'where this monument of soldiers' gallantry and endurance can be placed without being a nuisance'. The Commission Chairman, John Wrafter, duly instructed his secretary: 'Write asking for a site within the barrack grounds,[13] and we will remove it ourselves'.[14] And moved it was, because on an ordnance survey map from 1907, there it is, the now unwanted trophy, clearly marked just inside the front wall on the right as you enter the barracks.

Now, maybe I am suffering from False Memory Syndrome but I'm convinced that, way back in the early 1950's, I saw that cannon on the *left* side as you enter the barracks. From people I mentioned this to, I've got a mixed reaction; some nodded in remembrance; others shook their heads and looked sideways at me. So, am I imagining this? Apparently not. On the lawn of the Army Apprentice School (formerly Devoy Barracks) on the Newbridge road out of Naas, there once stood a cannon, 'dating back to the Crimean days'. It was, the *Leinster Leader* report continued,[15] 'procured from a redundant barracks in the midlands' but I have been able to ascertain that it came, in fact, from Portlaoise Garda barracks in 1956.[16] In 1998, the Apprentice School was relocated[17] to the Curragh Camp and, much to the dismay of Naas Urban District Council,[18] the gun went with it.

In 2014, I visited the Curragh Camp and yes, there in McDonagh barracks stands an imposing Russian twenty-four pounder naval gun,[19] made in Petrozavodsk in 1831, captured at Sevastopol and, until the emergence of proof to the contrary, the reason, I believe, for the celebrations in Market Place, Maryborough on that summer's day in 1858.

> Their's not to reason why,
> Their's but to do and die;
> Into the valley of Death
> Rode the six hundred.

NOTES

1. From the Town Commission's letter to Lord Panmure printed in the *Leinster Express*. Today, the letter seems woefully obsequious.
2. *Leinster Express*. December 12, 1857. Maryborough was far from being the only beneficiary of His Lordship's munificence: more than twenty cannon were presented to various Irish towns and cities. A full list can be found in *Crimean War guns in Ireland*. N. St. John Hennessy. *The Irish Sword*, The Journal of the Military History Society of Ireland. Vol. XIX, No. 78.
3. *Ibid*.
4. For much of the 19th century, the Pilsworth family was prominent in the town. As far back as 1824, for instance, a William Pilsworth was an apothecary and Inspector of Maryborough Gaol. In 1837 his namesake was Postmaster and, in 1851, an X. Pilsworth was Treasurer of the local Masonic Lodge. I have been unable to establish exact connections between these men, but what I am sure of is that, from the 1830's until his death in 1871, the owner of the business on the corner of Main Street and Church Street was Thomas Pilsworth, apothecary and Chairman of the Town Commission.
5. *Leinster Express*. July 31,1858.
6. *Ibid*.
7. *History Ireland*. Volume 11, Issue 1 (spring, 2003).
8. Joseph Templing died in 1884 and is buried in the Ridge Cemetery (known locally as 'the Bernridge'). His brother, James, incidentally, was for many years a grocer and baker at No. 41, Quality Row (Grattan Street today). Both he and his wife Esther (née Kearney) died in the 1920's and are buried in St. Peter & Paul's Cemetery. I am much indebted to Eamonn Hart – direct descendant of the Templings – for my information on the family.
9. In the absence of documentary evidence, I cannot be absolutely

certain that Mrs. Grennan was indeed the mother of Private Edward Grennan, but based on what knowledge I do have, I think it is reasonable to assume that such was the case. For more about Private Grennan, see *Forgotten Heroes. The Charge of the Light Brigade.* Roy Dutton. InfoDial Limited. 2007.

10.   *Melbourne Argus*, reprinted in *Nelson Evening Mail*, Nelson, New Zealand, October 24, 1896. The article features Edward Grennan's eyewitness account of what happened at Balaclava.

11.   *Redpath's Weekly. A Journal of Pure and Sparkling Literature for the Family.* New York. Number 403, 1884.

12.   *Leinster Express.* July 31,1858.

13.   Built in 1808 as an infantry barracks, it was subsequently the head-quarters of the 4th Battalion, Leinster Regiment. During the Civil War it was briefly held by the IRA before becoming an Irish Free State Army barracks. It has been a Garda Síochána barracks since the 1930's.

14.   *Freeman's Journal.* Dublin. February 4,1880.

15.   *Leinster Leader.* Naas. September 9, 2009.

16.   Information related by the late Colonel Con Costello to Reg Darling, historian, the Curragh Camp, who confirmed it to me. Colonel Costello was in charge of the detail transporting the cannon from Portlaoise to Naas. It was so heavy that, en route, it fell through the floor of the truck and 'reinforcements' had to be called to reinstate it.

17.   Kildare County Council offices occupy the site today.

18.   Chairman Paddy Behan was 'outraged and deeply disappointed' by the decision. See http://kildare.ie/knn/newsweeknov2198.htm.

19.   According to the *King's County Chronicle* of July 21, 1858, the Maryborough cannon was a 48 pounder, but that seems to be a mistake because a comprehensive list compiled by N. St. John Hennessy (Note 2 above), contains no such cannon, but does include the Naas 24 pounder.

SIX MARYBOROUGH HOTELS

After much wrangling by landowners for compensation – a claim by one local clergyman was promptly dismissed as extortionate[1] – the Great Southern and Western Railway came to the town in June, 1847. Within a few years, The Railway Hotel of Maryborough, owned by John Mathews, opened for business on the corner of Main Street and Railway Street (formerly known as Church Lane). John Mathews had been in business here since at least 1845, so it is likely that his establishment was simply renamed to take advantage of the railway's arrival.

After his death in 1872, the hotel remained closed until April, 1877 when his son Henry reopened it under the name Mathews' Railway & Commercial Hotel. The *Freeman's Journal* announced that the new premises were 'completely and most comfortably furnished, and fitted up throughout in the best modern style'. Henry Mathews, it added, hoped to 'merit the patronage so liberally bestowed on my late father'. The hotel offered their customers more than food, drink and a good night's sleep: in the 1890's, for instance, the Irish-American Dental Surgeons were there on alternate Mondays to look after all your dental requirements.

Henry's brother, Thomas, was better known as an historian than hotelier. His works include *An Account of the*

O'Dempseys: Chiefs of Clan Maliere (1903) and *The O'Neills of Ulster* (1907). He also contributed to a history of the Queen's County and County Kildare, serialised in the *Leinster Express* (1897-99) and published in book form in 1901. More than a century later, it was reissued as part of a three-volume set, complied by Patrick F. Meehan and published by Camira Publications, Portlaoise.

After Henry Mathews' death in 1910, the premises became a sucession of public houses owned by the Fitzpatrick family, Patrick McLogan, Phil Lewis and Michael Ryan. In 2006, the building was completely demolished and replaced by Boylesports.com. The upper storey houses a casino and Caesar's Card Club.

Φ

Just a few doors down Main Street stands O'Loughlin's Hotel. In the 1850's, this was an RIC barracks, but was subsequently acquired by the Aird family who, in June, 1904, opened the Central Hotel. According to an early advertisement, it was 'most comfortable and up-to-date in every respect, with hot and cold baths and perfect sanitary arrangements.' In 1911, the manageress was twenty-one-year-old Mary Angela Aird, daughter of James Joseph and Mary Aird who we'll meet again further down the street.

On Saturday, May 15, 1915, the *Leinster Express* reported that George Bernard Shaw, 'the distinguished litterateur and a party of friends who had been on a motoring tour in the West of Ireland, visited Maryborough on Monday evening, and remained overnight, staying at Aird's Central Hotel'. GBS had, in fact, a prior connection with Maryborough when, during World War I, he was invited to address an Anti-Vaccination meeting in the town. He declined, but in a letter to the organisers, he strongly advocated 'cleanliness and careful sanitation' as an alternative to vaccination against smallpox. In an earlier letter to the Irish Anti-Vaccination League in May, 1911, his pronouncements were somewhat less measured: 'vaccination is nothing short of attempted murder.'

Some might describe heavyweight boxing as attempted murder, but the hundreds of young people who, in February, 1932, turned up to gawk at another famous visitor to Aird's, hardly shared that sentiment. 'The Gorgeous Gael', Jack Doyle, was a boxer, singer, film star (and, years into the future, the subject of Jimmy McCarthy's great song *The Contender*). Whatever about his talents outside the ring, the *Leinster Express* writer was certainly impressed by this 'fine type, physically' and his 'quiet, rather reserved manner.'

A 1919 newspaper advertisement announced that Aird's had electric light and 'an installation of electric bells' powered by an oil-driven generator in the yard behind the hotel. Their Maryborough Electricity Works was one of more than 150 separate 'mini' electricity systems in the country at the time. Some were run by local authorities, others by entrepreneurs like J. J. Aird.

The family was also involved in the motor car trade and, in the 1920's, their Central Garage was situated at the rear of the hotel. 'Open night and day', the garage sold Clyno cars – at the time, the third largest car manufacturer in the UK after Austin and Morris – but warned that all cars were driven at their owner's risk!

In 1933, Dan Breen, Fianna Fáil TD and author of *My Fight for Irish Freedom*, a memoir of his time in the IRA, was having a drink in Aird's when he was approached by a local man. Words were exchanged, a blow was struck and, to cut a long story short, the encounter continued out on Main Street where more fisticuffs ensued, a gun was produced but not fired, and the local man – a relation of my own – ended up in hospital.

The Aird family continued to run the business until the late 1960's, after which it had a variety of owners and names. In the 1970's and '80's, it was Henderson's and, in the early 90's, The Regency. The hotel – which, for a short while in 1997, featured an incongruous thatched porch on Main Street – is today (January, 2016) owned by Declan O'Loughlin, well-known in GAA circles as a selector with the Laois Senior Footballers during the Mick O'Dwyer era (2003-2006) when the county won its first Leinster Senior title since 1946.

In a display case in the hotel bar, there's a set of Prescription Books from Bolger's Medical Hall which once stood next door. They make for fascinating reading: the medically-minded among you will pore over the details of obsolete concoctions, while someone like myself will have great interest in the names of townspeople long gone. But one thing that did catch my non-scientific eye was how often glyco-heroin was prescribed for the nuns in the Presentation Convent. Let me quickly add that heroin, mixed with glycerine – and often, sugar or spices – to make it more palatable, was widely used not only as a painkiller, but as a remedy for coughs, asthma, and pneumonia.

Φ

Next we move into the Lower Square. In March, 1836, William Power announced[2] that he had opened a new hotel in Main Street,[3] and hoped, 'by strict attention to the comfort of those who may favour his establishment, to merit a share of public patronage'.

The new hotel attracted the great and the good of Irish society (including, for instance, Lord and Lady Clarina, Sir William and Lady Chatterton, and Robert Otway-Cave, MP for Tipperary). It also became a popular venue for various meetings, from that of Upper Ossory Farming Society to what, in April, 1837, the local paper called 'the most influential and numerous meeting of the Conservative gentry of the Queen's County that ever assembled on any former occasion'. Their aim was to 'ensure the return of Sir Charles Coote and Hon. Thos. Vesey at the next election'.[4]

On a lighter note, the story goes that some guests were enjoying a game of cards when a terrified waiter burst in, mumbling about the ghostly noises he heard coming from underneath the hotel. Our intrepid travellers adjourned to the cellars where, sure enough, they heard what our patriotic narrator was quick to reassure us was not the 'diabolical screech' of the Scotch pipes, but the bleating of the old-fashioned Irish bagpipes. The story, which goes on to embrace a mixture of legend, historical detail, and the town's oldest inhabitant, is too long to recount here, but you can find it in *Fort and Town of Maryborough*, originally printed in the *Leinster Express* in the 1890's and reissued as part of the aforementioned three-volume set from Camira Publications.

The next owner was Thomas Kelly but by the time of Griffith's Valuation (taken in Queen's County in the late 1840's/early1850's), the premises were vacant. In March, 1857, the hotel was put up for sale by order of the Sheriff, James Butler. The purchaser was Simon Kelly[5] who, in his will, left the business in trust to two local priests, Rev. John Doyle and Rev. Michael Comerford. Clergymen could not apply for a transfer of the licence; legal arguments ensued, and the upshot was that the 'extensive lucrative wholesale and retail Spirit and Wine Trade formerly known as Power's Hotel' wasn't put on the market until 1884[6].

The premises and licence were bought by Mrs. Mary Aird. She, the former Mary Fitzpatrick from Maryborough, was the wife of William Aird from Glasthule in Dublin. After his early death from TB, Mary and her only child, James Joseph (born 1862) returned to live with her sister Catherine Delaney who had a shop at 31, Main Street. Time passed:

James Joseph learned his trade with Keeley's Hardware and Timber Merchants in Tullamore, and eventually opened his own business in the building his mother had bought in 1884. Selling everything from furniture, saddles and glass, to coffins, groceries and farm machinery, J. J. Aird, General Merchant and Auctioneer, was, for many years, one of the town's most prominent businessmen.

When Aird's eventually closed in the late 1930's, the building was put to many different uses. It became the headquarters of the Fire Brigade (and residence of the Chief Fire Officer) and the local Red Cross. After World War 2, it was from offices here that the Marshall Plan was administered locally. Since then, the partitioned premises have housed everything from a hairdressing salon, photographic studio and discount store to a newsagent, Wimpy Bar and Halal foodstore.

Φ

Continue down Lower Main Street and you will see, on the southern side, the derelict County Hotel. Dating from the early nineteenth century, this once-fine building has been an eyesore for many years, a situation exacerbated by a fire in June, 2015.

In 1850, the premises were known as Leinster House and belonged to Patrick Quigley. In 1870, the license was transferred to Patrick Doran who, according to the *Leinster Express* of July 9, was 'a very respectable young man whose friends had come to set him up in trade'. In the 1890's, Leinster House became the Leinster Hotel which *A Guide to Christmas Shopping*, published by the same paper in 1901, praised thus: 'during the few years in which it has been open, it has developed an extensive connection... is fitted with every modern comfort, and caters well for its visitors.'

Elizabeth, Patrick Doran's daughter and manageress of the establishment, must have been well pleased.

As well as being a hotelier and publican, Mr. Doran was also a Justice of the Peace, member of the Town Commission and the Irish Republican Brotherhood. In 1881 he spent three months in Naas Gaol for suspected Land League activities. On his release that August, bands turned out to greet him at the railway station and he was borne through the town on a carriage drawn by his supporters. The *Leinster Express* report reads like a parody of Christ's entry into Jerusalem: 'Some convenient plantation was availed of, and whole trees were placed in parallel lines opposite Mr. Doran's door through which, as an avenue, he entered his house'.

Patrick Doran was succeeded by his son and namesake and, after the latter's untimely death in 1919, the hotel was acquired by the Butler family. In August, 1939, the premises were bought by Charles Delaney who was also active in political life – member of the Town Commission, County Council, and numerous committees – but an unsuccessful Fine Gael candidate in the General Election of 1943.

In 1961, Fionán and Kathleen Bracken acquired the business and throughout the 1960's and '70's, the County Hotel was the venue of the weekly and extremely popular Rugby Club Dance. In 1976, it also boasted an off-licence and gift shop where you would find 'a large and varied selection of jewellery' and, surprisingly, 'grandfather clocks available on order'.

After the Brackens left the hotel in August, 1982, it was taken over by Danny Dempsey and advertised as the 'No. 1 Spot for Entertainment in the Midlands', hosting such attractions as Eddie's Disco Roadshow ('Girls free up to 11.30.') and 'Direct from London! Miss Wet T-Shirt'.

Stay on the same side, and head back up the street until you come to Lethean, which faces directly into Church Street. This was originally Fallon's Hotel, founded in 1798 and described by Slater's *Directory of Ireland* (1846) as 'a family, commercial and posting establishment[7] of great and long-standing respectability'. In September 1815, *Finn's Leinster Journal* reported the death of Matilda Fallon, 'wife of inn-keeper Patrick Fallon', who was 'sincerely and deservedly lamented by a numerous family and acquaintance'.

On January 6, 1839, the so-called Night of the Big Wind (*Oíche na Gaoithe Móire*), gales of up to 115 mph swept across the country, causing widespread damage and several hundred deaths. Queen's County was spared the worst of its ravages but, Fallon's Hotel, like other buildings in the town did suffer substantial damage. However traumatic that was for the owner, it hardly compared with what he witnessed on June 11, 1845. On that day, the 13th Light Dragoons halted in the town and their commanding officer stopped in the hotel. When he didn't appear the next day, Mr. Fallon and others forced open his door which was locked from the inside, and found Major W. D. Hamilton 'lying on the broad of his back weltering in his blood'. As reported in *The Cork Examiner*,[8] 'the unhappy gentleman had cut the arteries of his sword arm with a razor. Surgical aid was in immediate attendance and the arteries were tied up. Recovery is doubtful'. The Major, a native of Bath, was only twenty-one years of age. But there was a happy ending; a subsequent report announced that 'The Major is better. The surgeon of the regiment, Dr. Young, remains up with him'.

In 1847, John McEvoy became the new owner and, after extensive alterations, the premises reopened as the Maryborough Hotel. (This is probably the same John

McEvoy who, in the 1850's, ran the 'refreshment rooms' at the railway station). He also operated the mail coaches from Maryborough to Waterford: after his contract expired in 1858, an advertisement in the *Freeman's Journal* offered for sale 'two light coaches and twenty-five prime mail coach horses, most of them well adapted for Gentlemen's Carriages, having both blood, youth and action'. Four years later, the hotel closed down and its furniture, not to mention one cow and ten cocks of hay – were auctioned off.

The business was acquired by John Gaze, an auctioneer in the town. The *Leinster Express* announced that the new owner 'begs to inform the public that he has purchased the interest in this old established hotel' and that 'no expense will be spared in making it a house in which the nobility, clergy, gentry and commercial gentlemen visiting Maryborough will find accommodation such as cannot be excelled in any provincial town in the country'. John Gaze was succeeded in the business by his son, Francis Hinds Gaze. (Their surname, incidentally, will still be familiar to those who remember Gaze and Jessop's hardware shop in Church Street).

In October, 1875, *The Irish Times* advertised a meeting in the hotel 'to advance the cause of Home Rule, Tenant Right and Union amongst Irishmen'. Many dignitaries were expected to attend, among them Isaac Butt and Charles Stewart Parnell. The meeting was scheduled for 1 pm and if you wanted to stay on for the Banquet at six, you could return to Dublin on the Night Mail at 2.13 am. I don't know how 'relaxed' was the post-prandial socialising, but six years later, there was definitely plenty of noise around the hotel. Cattle seized in lieu of unpaid rent from tenants on the estate of Richard Warburton of Garryhinch were being auctioned, and the anger of the crowd – to say nothing of the disruptive music played by local bands locked outside the yard – made for a very tense atmosphere.[9]

A quick diversion. In September, 1877, Francis Gaze's name appeared in the *Freeman's Journal* for an altogether different reason. Those of us of a certain age will remember the disused corn mill on Green Mill Lane, off the Green Road. We especially remember the notorious archway there, and some of us may have heard the story about it being haunted by a headless horseman...

On September 26, Thomas Wilson was driving down the lane – in a horse and car owned by Francis Gaze – when he underestimated the height of the arch. An eyewitness and some millworkers lifted him on to the car and brought him to Mr. Gaze's hotel. The latter had him conveyed to Dr. Jacob's, but it was too late; the unfortunate man was dead.

In 1886, the proposed sale of the hotel to George Dimond[10] fell through but, the following year, the lease came up for sale again (...'ten bedrooms, five sitting-rooms, kitchen, scullery, wc etc. To a businessman it presents a rare opportunity of making a fortune in this rapidly rising and prosperous town...'[11]) and was bought by ex-RIC man, Patrick Kelly and his wife Margaret who renamed it the Hibernian Hotel.[12] A member of the Town Commission, Mr. Kelly was also a staunch Parnellite and prominent in the Land League.

In 1904, the Lord Lieutenant, the Earl of Dudley – familiar to readers of James Joyce's *Ulysses* – had lunch in the hotel. A less rarefied guest was Gene Tunney, former World Heavyweight Boxing Champion who stopped here in August, 1954. In his book *From an Irish Market Town*, Joe Rogers recalls getting 'quite a decent tip just for carrying his suitcase to the car.'

Patrick Kelly died in 1929 but the hotel remained in the Kelly family until the 1970's. In 1962, during the aftermath of Princess Margaret's controversial visit to the de Vesci estate in Abbeyleix, the hotel was used as the press centre for the assembled media.[13]

Kelly's Hotel gave me memories I'll never forget. In the mid-1960's, record hops – which we, of course, advertised as 'Happenings' – were held in a small room at the back. That little venue was a favourite haunt of those of us – decked out in our fabbest gear, man – too young and definitely too hip to be caught groovin' to showbands. With a clarity that is luminous, I recall the excitement of browsing LP covers ('Far out, man!'), sorting through singles and, not least, acting nonchalant for the girls. To paraphrase a David Bowie lyric, it was ragged and naive, it was Heaven. And most of all it was *ours*.

During the 1970's, the hotel was refurbished to include a brand new 'olde-worlde' Tudor Room ('Why not treat yourself and your wife to an evening out?') which, in the next decade, gave way to Swanky's Lounge Bar. The owners at this stage were Fionán and Kathleen Bracken who we've already met in the County Hotel. My abiding memories of this time are of the regular meetings we – *Laois Literary Society* – held here, and the night (November 1, 1986) Paul Durcan gave a reading as part of the *Meitheal na Samhna* Laois Arts Festival. This was literature as many had never heard it before; poetry in sometimes furious, sometimes shocking, sometimes hilarious, overdrive...

The premises subsequently became Bellamy's pub and off-licence under the guiding hand of Jim Birch, former manager of both the Killeshin and Montague Hotels. At one stage (1990), it took to advertising itself as *Áras* Bellamy.

In August, 1999, Bellamy's became Lethean Gastro Pub and Cafe Bar owned by the Watchorne family. According to its own publicity, Lethean had a 'super cool beer garden' and was 'the only place in Laois to serve Sunday brunch'. And if that wasn't enough to make you forget all your cares,[14] the venue also hosted regular Open Mic sessions where many of the town's hopefuls got their first blast of stage fright and applause.

I came into Fallon's on a coach horse but I'll leave on its more humble relation. On July 25, 1912, a show for working donkeys was held in the hotel yard. Over twenty animals were exhibited but, as *The Irish Times* explained, 'owing to farming and turf-drawing operations many could not be exhibited'. After the presentation of prizes – awarded for good condition and the care shown to the animals – the donkeys paraded *via* Bull Lane, Main Street and Market Square up to the Town Hall. And on that note I'll trot off into the sunset. Well, maybe just as far as next door…

Built between 1810 and 1830, this fine three-storey building is one of the oldest on the Main Street. From at least 1824, Jonathon Hill was a grocer and haberdasher here. He died in 1849 and was succeeded by – his wife? daughter? – Frances. The property, incidentally, was leased from Mrs. Sophia J. Stoker who was more than likely related to the Stoker family from Ballyroan. One of that family, Bartholomew, was once a highly-regarded portrait painter. He died in 1788, aged only twenty-five, and was interred with his parents in Old St. Peter's Churchyard in Railway Street. More recent members of the family lie in St. Peter's in the Market Square. So, what's the connection between 'our' Mrs. Stoker and the creator of Dracula? There's a bit of research to get your teeth into.

In the 1860's, the property belonged to grocer and spirit dealer, John Boland and his wife Catherine and, from at least 1879, the latter ran a Temperance Hotel here.[15] In 1901, what the *Leinster Express* called 'that old resting place known as Boland's Hotel' closed for good. The premises lay vacant for some time before becoming a butcher's shop – owned by my great-granduncle, Joseph Dunne – which continued in business for almost seventy years. More recent occupants include a hardware shop, a bookshop, the Herb House (which also offered acupuncture and massage) and a veritable fashion show of clothes shops. Today (January, 2016), the building houses Peavoy auctioneers, valuers and estate agents.

I'll conclude with a few random notes which will be the basis for further research. If you have any information on any of the following establishments, please let me know.

A lease, dated May 16, 1710, between the burgomaster and bailiffs of Maryborough and Bartholomew Senior the Younger, refers to a premises known as the Ship.[16] In the most landlocked county in Ireland!

On April 17, 1792, the *Freeman's Journal* carried a notice for the Black Bull Inn 'in the town of Maryborough… held by the late Mr. Andrew Graves… the house is excellent, the rear extensive and the standing, one of the best in Ireland for that line of business…'

In the late 18th century there was an inn on the Turnpike (Limerick) Road at Boughlone owned by the Widow Dowling. 'Constant running water near the house, and a good turf bog within half a mile of it, the stabling and offices are good, and the whole well situated for carrying on any manufacture'.[17]

The story goes that the former Fitzgibbon residence on Tower Hill was once the Swan Hotel, with an image of a swan in the fanlight. It was owned by a Mrs. Maguire.

And finally, Quinn's Hotel, on the corner of Factory Lane and Grattan Street was, apparently, more of a doss-house than anything else. According to local legend, for a penny you could sleep on your back, for a ha'penny on your side, and for a farthing, slumped over a rope. Sweet dreams.

NOTES

1. As reported in *The Cork Examiner*. September 2, 1846.
2. *Leinster Express*. March 12, 1836.
3. Officially No. 22, Main Street, aka the Lower Square.
4. The political fortunes of both men may be traced in *The Members of Parliament for Laois & Offaly (Queen's and King's Counties) 1801-1918*. Patrick F. Meehan. The Leinster Express (1972) Ltd. Portlaoise. 1983.
5. Listed in Slater's *Directory of Ireland* (1870) as a grocer and publican. I have been unable to establish any connection between 'the two Kellys'.
6. *Leinster Express*. June 14, and October 18, 1884.
7. A posting hotel was one of a series of establishments along a route for furnishing relays of men and horses for carrying mail.
8. *The Cork Examiner*. June 11, 1845.
9. Adding to the tension was the presence of the notorious Morris Goddard, Captain Charles Boycott's solicitor who had organised a workforce from Ulster to break the boycott on the eponymous estate at Lough Mask. He was in Maryborough representing the Property Defence Association – established by landlords to oppose the Land League – and carried 'a stout blackthorn stick' and what was described as 'an ominous protrusion of his coat skirt at the left hip'. (It was the Property Defence Association, incidentally, that devised the battering ram as a means of expediting evictions.) The events of March 15, 1881 in Gaze's Hotel were recalled in 'Window on the Past' in *The Irish Press* of March 15, 1962.
10. In 1892, he opened Dimond's Medical Hall where Breslin's pharmacy stands today. George Dimond was also Assistant Registrar of Births, Marriages and Deaths, Secretary of the Queen's County Infirmary (now Grattan Business Centre on the Dublin Road) and, for thirty-two years, the apothecary for the asylum. The Dimond family, who lived in Rosetta on the Dublin Road (or Dublin *Street* as it was called in the early years of the last century), eventually emigrated to Australia.
11. *Freeman's Journal*. October 1, 1887.
12. That name is still visible on the building today, but well into living memory, the hotel was always known locally as 'Kelly's'. Patrick Kelly also owned – since at least 1888 – a substantial farm machinery business (on the site of the present Wesley Terrace and Heritage Hotel Fitness Centre) which evolved into what is still remembered as 'Kellys the Foundry'. The company specialised in haysheds and, though it is long gone, its blue-and-white sign – Erected by Ptk. Kelly & Co. Ltd., Portlaoise – can still be seen on many structures throughout the country.

13. http://www.itnsource.com/shotlist/BHC_ITN/1965/01/27/X27016502/?v=0&a=1

14. Lethean refers to Lethe, one of the five rivers of Hades. Whoever drank from it experienced complete forgetfulness. Lethean is certainly the most Classically-connected pub in the town; Dona, the name of the former manageress, is the Latin word for *gifts*.

15. Temperance Hotels – and the spread of tea houses and coffee houses – were a product of the 19th century Temperance Movement. In the late 1830's, Father Theobald Mathew (1790-1856), known as The Apostle of Temperance, led a crusade against the evils of alcohol. The Movement became enormously popular and it is estimated that, by the mid-1840's, almost three million people – half of the adult population of Ireland – had taken the Pledge: *I promise to abstain from all intoxicating drinks except used medicinally and by order of a medical man and to discountenance the cause and practice of intemperance.*

    After High Mass in SS Peter & Paul's on June 6, 1840, Fr. Mathew preached in a nearby field. Such was the fervour he inspired that a near-riot ensued with invalids trampled, and the reverend reformer himself thrown from his platform. Nevertheless, tens of thousands from far and near took the Pledge over that week-end.

16. Report from *Commission on Municipal Corporations in Ireland*. Inquiry held in September, 1833 before John Colhoun and Henry Baldwin.

17. Advertisement in *Finn's Leinster Journal*. January 29, 1772.

MUSIC FROM GRATTAN STREET

Throughout the first half of the twentieth century, one family in particular was responsible for keeping our town on the musical map of Ireland...

Φ

'So high did the flames arise in the now dark sky that they were seen for miles in the country... Hundreds, and amongst them some of the most respectable inhabitants, vied with each other in seeing who would carry most water... One of the greatest dangers that ever threatened the town of Maryborough was overcome and conquered.'

That is how the *Freeman's Journal*[1] reported the response to the fire that, one summer's evening in 1870, raged through the rear of Phelan's grocery, public house and hardware premises at No. 74, Main Street. It destroyed large quantities of hay and turf and threatened to spread along the street. The paper went on to mention that a next-door neighbour 'particularly distinguished himself: when the fire was at its very height, he jumped upon an outhouse next the flaming straw... the thatch was quickly torn from the roof... Mr. Bannan was in evident danger, smashing through the rafters and woodwork, and so cutting off communication from that end.'

In the 1880's, the same Tobias Bannan acquired No. 16,

Market Square. On the night of the 1901 census, he was at home with his wife Maria and their four sons. The modest description (Carpenter, Shopkeeper) on that Census Form understates his many talents and activities: he was also an undertaker, water diviner, a sinker of wells, a borer of pumps, a blender and bottler of whiskey. As well as all that, he found time to erect a calvary in the local cemetery and build the crib which, for many years, adorned the parish church at Christmastime.

Tobias Bannan died in April, 1915 and the business was continued by his son George (1890-1944) whose versatility – as is evident from his newspaper advertisement – matched his late father's: 'Undertaker, Building Contractor and General merchant. Wood and Metal Pumps supplied. Saw Mills, All sorts of Joinery, Plumbing of all descriptions.'

I don't know if musician could be added to the list of Tobias and George Bannan's accomplishments, but the latter's brother Richard (b. 1880) was certainly blessed with the gift of music. At the *Feis Ceoil* in Dublin in May, 1908, he won the medal for the althorn: he also played the violin and subsequently went on to form a small band with his wife Elizabeth, née Cullen.[2] She, too, was a very accomplished musician – in 1912, she obtained a London School of Music degree – and the story goes that it was during auditions for the band that Richard met and fell in love with her. After their marriage, Richard and Elizabeth lived at No. 32, Grattan Street where all their children grew up.

The Bannans accompanied the silent films in Paul Delany's newly-opened Electric Cinema and, in later years, with other family members, formed one of the leading provincial dance orchestras. In 1924, Richard leased a large shed on Station Road from my grandaunt Mary Anne Hargroves, removed the loft, put in a new floor, and organised dance classes with music by the family band. The venue was initially advertised as the Terpsichore[3] Hall – a name hardly guaranteed to trip off the tongues or inspire the feet of local dancers – but that was soon abandoned, and the hall become well-known as simply 'Bannan's'. From the *Leinster Express* of November 11, 1925: 'The floor is in excellent order, and with the Bannan Orchestra dispensing their celebrated musical contributions ad lib, everything augurs well for the future of the dancing fraternity in the capital town of Leix.' Bannan's Hall continued as a dancehall (and latterly, an amusement centre run by Jim Cully, reputedly Ireland's tallest man at the time) into the 1960's. Since 1969, the building has been occupied by Reliable House Furnishers.

In April, 1946, while visiting her daughter Nancy, a boarder in the Brigidine Convent, Mountrath, Elizabeth Bannan suddenly became seriously ill and died the next day. Richard died in 1957. Their children inherited their great gift for music: probably the best-remembered of them today is Toby (1916-1975) who led a very popular dance orchestra.

His first band in the 1930's was known as Toby Bannan and his Revellers and, on and off for forty years, he played all over Ireland, leading everything from trios and quartets to augmented dance bands. As well as the violin, Toby also played the saxophone, banjo and guitar. In the 1940's – when the electric guitar was little more than a decade old – his solos on the electric Hawaiian guitar were attracting special attention.[4] He specialised in seasonal hotel residencies and was clearly held in high esteem by his peers: I have seen notices by musicians advertising themselves as 'ex-Toby Bannan'. One such, incidentally, was a trumpet player Lewis Armstrong (who wasn't from New Orleans!)

At different stages, various of his siblings were members of the band; most often, pianist and Hammond organist Marie who, at a young age, won prizes for her performance of classical pieces on the piccolo; Paddy, who played the accordion, piano and double bass, and Margaret (known as Pixie), a proficient drummer and frequent guest vocalist. They were occasionally joined by another sister, Nancy, on double bass. Other local members included Jimmy Meehan – stalwart of the Ballyroan Brass Band and fondly remembered by many townies for his atmospheric trumpet on special occasions in SS Peter and Paul's Church – and his brother Jack from Ballyroan.

Easter Sunday Night, 1943, saw one of the highlights in Portlaoise's Social Calendar: the official opening of the Coliseum Ballroom on the New Road.[5] Despite bad weather, more than five hundred danced the night away to the music of Toby Bannan's Orchestra. I can only imagine how he felt playing for such a grand occasion in front of a big crowd in his hometown. I don't know if the dancers that night were treated to an example of the wit he was renowned for. On one occasion, after discovering that some dancers had got in without paying, he approached the microphone: 'The next dance, ladies and gentlemen, will be a snakedance, and those of ye that snaked in without paying can snake back out again...'

Toby's career continued right into the 1970's. In June, 1970, his resident orchestra at the Bray Head Hotel featured female vocalists The Bannanettes, and in October of the following year, he was performing in Leitrim 'direct from a successful English cabaret tour'. In July, 1974, a *Sunday Independent* review of one of his final performances in the Crofton Hotel, Bray, marvelled at how his band could swing effortlessly from 'hokey-pokey to disco thunder'! In 1975, Toby Bannan died at home in Bray.

So far, I have been unable to discover recordings by any of Toby Bannan's various bands. I know that his orchestra played a mixture of jazz standards and popular tunes of the day, and I can guess at what they sounded like, but should anyone reading this know of any Bannan recordings, I would love to hear from you. But I have been able to locate an informal home tape made by the family in 1959. The occasion was the imminent departure to America of Toby's sister Nancy,[6] and the tape's mixture of music and personal greetings was intended as a gift for relations in Connecticut. The sound quality is far from perfect and, from speaking to many people who remember the bands in their heyday, I believe that the music conveys little idea of Toby and Marie at their professional best. If you would like to hear excerpts from this recording, please go to

http://www.portlaoisepictures.com/bannan4.htm

NOTES

1. August 2, 1870.
2. Her nephew, Christy Cullen from Kilbricken, is today a well-known songwriter, composer of our unofficial anthem *Lovely Laois* and many other popular songs.
3. In Greek mythology, one of the nine muses, goddess of choral music and dance.
4. *The Tuam Herald*. March 17, 1945.
5. Built by contractor Paddy Mathews – he also had a pub in the Market Square – and owned by a consortium of local businessmen, the Coliseum Ballroom stood near where the New Road/JFL Avenue roundabout is today. It soon became the most popular venue in the town, hosting everything from regular dances, Gala Balls and *Feis Mór Laoise*, to fashion shows, variety shows and children's Fancy Dress competitions. In 1962, it was renovated and renamed Danceland.
6. A talented visual artist, she is still alive and well in Eureka, California. I am much indebted to her for the help she gave me in the preparation of this article.

TOWN HALL ENTERTAINMENT 1886-1945

There you are, a hundred years ago, a dashing young chap about town, all set for a splendid night out. Your first port of call is Maryborough Toilet Saloon on Main Street where, under the expert hands of brothers Charles and Albert Knapton, you'll have your hair washed, cut, and pomaded. Then maybe a fortifying pint of Bass across the street in the Hibernian and, off you go, sashaying towards the Square and the Grand Concert in the Town Hall; a spring in your step and a certain young lady on your mind...

Where the statue of the Blessed Virgin now presides over the Market Square, once stood – from 1803 – the town's Market House. Over the years, it fell into disuse and by the 1880's was described as 'a prominent and unsightly object'.[1] In 1885, the Town Commission advertised a competition for the transformation of the building, and the talents of the winning architect, John Hampden Shaw, and contractor, George Crampton, resulted in a magnificent new Town Hall which, in January of the following year, was officially handed over to the Commissioners.

The ground floor consisted of a boardroom with adjoining lavatory, a weighmaster's office, storerooms, and housing for two fire engines. Upstairs, reached by a wide stone stairway, and through swinging doors panelled with coloured glass, was the assembly room/concert hall. This measured sixty-seven feet by twenty-two, and was fitted out, at the southern end, with a stage, gas-fired footlights, and dressing rooms. At the opposite end, a gallery was reached by way of stairs from a doorway at the rear of the building. The walls were painted French Grey and wainscotted with red pitch pine. The room was lit by six gothic windows and, when necessary, four gasaliers. It soon became the town's principal venue, hosting everything from light entertainment to heavyweight political meetings.

The first concert – to raise funds for the Catholic Young Men's Society – took place on February 3, 1886 and featured mostly local singers who, according to the local paper, were 'up to the average standard of amateurs'.[2] One of the soloists, incidentally, was P. A. Meehan, future Chairman of the County Council, MP, and grandfather of the late local historian Patrick F. (Frank) Meehan. Patrick Aloysius was also, on occasion, visited by the poetic muse: depending on your own sensibilities, this is either a rousing clarion call or a bit of harmless oul' doggerel:

The land for the people! Hurrah boys hurrah!
Justice and freedom and Erin go Bragh!
We'll rally round the flag, boys, we'll rally once again
Shouting the battle-cry of Freedom!

A month after that inaugural concert, a more exotic act appeared. On a European tour to raise funds for their college in Nashville,[3] the Fisk University Jubilee Singers, a 'troupe of coloured folk', performed their 'quaint music and rude poetry'[4] to a capacity audience. The evening's profit of £9.00 – roughly €800 in today's money – was divided between three local clergymen for distribution among the poor. The concert might also be seen as a local antidote to much late 19th century popular music that was absolutely polluted with poisonous racist sentiments. Two of the biggest hits of the period were *If the Man in the Moon were a Coon* and *All Coons look Alike to Me*. And the song that launched Al Jolson's career in 1911 was, believe it or not, *Paris is a Paradise for Coons*.

As the 20th century dawned, the second Boer War was raging in South Africa. On January 8, a concert was held in aid of the families of men engaged in the conflict. The programme combined the sentimental and the militaristic, and one of the performers in the latter category, Anaeas Lamont from Coote Street, was an interesting character. A Belfast Protestant, working as a bookkeeper in Odlum's Mill, he publicly expressed support for Home Rule and his respect for Catholics, especially the aforementioned Patrick A. Meehan.[5]

In February, 1901, the Maryborough Christy Minstrels Troupe put on a show whose repertoire of 'Nigger dialogues, conundrums and dances'[6] would certainly raise more than an eyebrow today. But if you wanted to get in shape for Christmas 1902, Madam Hayes was, so to speak, your only man. Her Dancing, Calisthenics and Deportment classes promised to have you tripping the light fantastic to the Waltz, the Skating Dance and the Berlin Polka.

If you liked to combine fisticuffs with your fancy footwork, December 29, 1911 would have been underlined in your diary. The evening began with a selection of music, and then a roped-in ring was set up on the stage. In his introduction, the MC, Mr. T. Tweedy – his surname will ring a bell with readers of *Ulysses* – stoutly defended the Art of Boxing ('not any more objectionable then hockey or croquet') and requested the crowd to be 'perfectly still during the bouts: they could cheer as much as they liked at their conclusion'. So, with formalities out of the way, the pugilists tore into each another, and a blow-by-blow account of their exertions subsequently appeared in the *Leinster Express*.[7] The boxing[8] ended with one of the contestants dancing a jig and a reel; the ring was dismantled, the seats cleared away and a most unusual, even surreal, night ended with 'a merry few hours spent by a large number of dancers to the music of the orchestra'.

Some of the Hall's biggest attractions in the early years of the century were film or 'animated pictures' shows. When the Irish Animated Picture Company visited in November, 1906, the local paper marvelled at how audiences, 'seated in a hall within a short distance from their residences in a small country town', could have 'placed before them the scenes that took place at, for instance, the Olympic sports in Athens last summer, or look upon the winter games of Norway and Canada'.[9] A few years later, both cineastes – did that word exist then? – and those of a religious persuasion flocked to the Hall to witness *The Passion Play of Oberammergau*.[10]

'To avoid crushing only a limited number of tickets will be isued'.[11] So stated the advertisement for two Promenade Concerts to raise funds for a new organ stop in St. Peter's Church. The featured musicians were the band of the 4th Leinster Regiment. The term, promenade, in this context, originally referred to outdoor concerts in 18th century London where listeners could stroll around while listening to the music. (Think Electric Picnic in fancy suits and gowns). Today, the term refers to the annual summer series of concerts in the Royal Albert Hall where Promenaders ('Prommers') pay reduced prices to stand.

In September, 1916, the star of a concert in aid of the Red Cross was none other than Percy French, the famous composer and performer, who began writing songs while working as a civil engineer – he often called himself 'an Inspector of Drains' – for the Board of Works in Cavan. Today, he is probably best remembered by Don McLean's version of the *The Mountains of Mourne*, but you'd be surprised by how many of his songs lie dormant at the back of your head.

The Hall hosted everything from Maryborough Brass Band's fundraiser for new instruments to a Bal Masqué organised by the Queen's County Hunt. In January, 1918, Owen Clark, The Man of Mystery and his Great Vaudeville Company guaranteed nothing less than a 'decapitation extraordinary,' while a Fancy Dress Ball on St. Stephen's Night, 1921 certainly did cause one particular local to lose the head. At one stage, the lights were turned off, and God knows what the dancers got up to in the dark, but in a letter to the *Nationalist and Leinster Times*, pseudonymous *Glana* feared nothing less than 'the heathen practices of Continental atheists'. His missive goes on to pour scorn on 'Old Grandfathers who might pass for Santa Clause, baldy heads, and old maids, musty and well-seasoned from the shelf, who may be seen nightly enjoying themselves on the floor'.[12] (Fashionistas among you may be interested to learn that prizewinners for their outfits on the night included a Mrs. O'Connell as Powder Puff, Mr. James Tyrrell as a Sandwichman, and Mr. R. G. H. Russell as Chin Chin Chow.)

Further up the cultural totem pole, perhaps, were the Abbey Players who, in October, 1912, presented plays by W. B. Yeats, Lady Gregory and William Boyle. Yeats's nationalist allegory, *Cathleen Ní Houlihan*, could hardly be further removed from another event in the Hall some years later; Royal Air Force Captain Alston's lecture, *A Pilot's Experience at the Front*, illustrated with 'thrilling lantern slides from the Western Front'.

One genre that never seemed to go down too well was Opera. In December, 1905, for instance, the Elster-Grime Company drew very small audiences. I don't know whether they were wildly optimistic, or the taste of Maryborough audiences had changed dramatically but, nine years later, the company was back for a week with five different operas. I could find no reference to how successful, or otherwise, that run was, or how the Flintoff Moore Grand Opera Company fared when they visited the town in January, 1930.

As might be expected, pantomimes were always guaranteed to put the proverbial bums on seats: in February, 1925, there was a different show for each of six nights. Also very popular were performers like the Carrickford Repertory Company whose programme, 'preceded by a Grand Concert and concluded by a laughable farce',[13] changed every night for a week in February, 1923.

In October, 1934, the long-forgotten Fintan Lalor String Band provided the music for a *ceilidhe* organised by the County Camogie Board. Despite the stormy weather, over 100 couples took the floor and dancing continued into the early hours. According to the *Kildare Observer*, Patrick McLogan MP made a most capable master of ceremonies, and the catering, in the hands of a ladies' committee, 'was admirably carried out'.

Entertainment continued right throughout the 1930's, but change was on the way. The new Coliseum Ballroom (1943) quickly became a rival attraction, but it is still surprising to read how swift was the Hall's apparent neglect and decline. In August, 1944, Councillor Thomas Territt complained to the County Manager: 'If tourists came to Portlaoighise they would be shocked to see such a building in the middle of the town. If a cow could be got up on the eave gutters she would get fine grazing in them'.[14]

In December, 1944, Equity Productions, a drama group from Dublin, arrived to fulfil a four-day engagement only to find the premises closed on them.[15] The axe fell a month later when, on foot of a surveyor's report, the Town Commission issued an order prohibiting the use of the Hall for public entertainments. I still find it shocking and very sad how such a lovely building was allowed to deteriorate so drastically: the report stated that there was no sanitary accommodation; the stairway was in a dangerous condition with numerous newels missing; flooring was missing from the balcony; all the windows were rotten and sheeted with canvas and sacking.

The next debate on the Hall's future included this exchange:

TOWN COMMISSIONER: It would be right to blow it out of the place and make room for modern transport. It is right in the way.

COUNTY MANAGER: I don't know; I have never heard of anyone running into it.

The Commissioners eventually agreed to allocate £500 for renovations, but before they could start any work, the entire matter was decided for them: on Thursday, March 15, 1945, the Town Hall was destroyed by fire. Shortly after five o'clock in the morning, Miss Mary-Jo McCormack (who lived in the Market Square, a stone's throw from the Hall) was awakened by loud noise and noticed a glare in her bedroom. Thinking her house was on fire, she called for her mother[16] who raised the alarm. The Fire Brigade arrived, but the building was already an inferno. The official report of the Fire Brigade was that the fire was accidental.

But the story didn't end there. The Commissioners continued to debate whether the burnt-out building should be reconstructed, or a new Hall built elsewhere. Never let it be said that our elected representatives lacked vision: under the headline AIRPORT FOR MARKET SQUARE, the *Leinster Express* of August 18, reported that one of the Town Commissioners had proposed building a new Town Hall on a different site because we 'must consider future transport problems. Where the old building now stands, a plane will probably be leaving for Dublin and another one for Cork'. A committee was appointed to find a site for a new edifice that would be 'a credit to the town'. Suggested locations included Lyster Lane, Factory Lane and the Lower Square but, like the Commissioner's airplane, none of these ever got off the ground.

The gutted building stood there for years. At one stage, an architect was consulted, plans drawn up, advertisements for tenders published and, on August 20, 1949, the local paper reported that work would soon commence on re-building the Town Hall. The very next day, a large piece of limestone fell from the top of the old building, narrowly missing two young locals. Such near-tragedy must have influenced what happened next: the Town Commissioners decided to abandon their plans for a new hall and also to demolish the old one and clear the site. The reason given was that, after considering the tenders, the Commisssioners decided that the estimated cost (£16,300) would place too heavy a burden on the ratepayers of the town. Demolition began in early October, 1949 and the *Leinster Express* poured lavish praise on the Commissioners for getting rid of 'that awful wreck in the Square'.

But the issue would still not go away. For almost twenty years, the Commission agonised over what was to be done with the unused Town Hall Fund (comprised of insurance payment and accumulated interest). Proposals included a Town Park on the Ridge Road and a playground in O'Moore Place, until it was eventually decided to hand over the money (£3,000) to the County Council towards the building of the town's first public swimming pool.[17]

It is appropriate that I conclude this article on the town's 'entertainment centre' with two pieces inspired by the building itself. As far as I'm aware – but apologies if I'm wrong, and any information will be gratefully received – the composer of the first is anonymous, while the second is the work of Michael J. McGlynn[18] and was published in the *Leinster Express* of December 15, 1945.

THE OLD TOWN HALL[19]

We've travelled Nature's wonderland in far-off foreign nations
We've taken part in fun galore and many celebrations
But weary are our footsteps now, they serve but to remind us
That the best of all was the old Town Hall and the girls we left
behind us.

To Granuaile we soon set sail across the briny ocean
We never thought the day would come when filled with deep
emotion
We stood to stare on the Market Square till the rays of the sun
did blind us
For we don't see at all the old Town Hall and the girls we left
behind us.

It stood out there on the Market Square so stately and
imposing
While poor old Joe*, God rest his soul, was there at every
closing
Oh where are the joys and where are the boys with friendship
ties still bind us
We were all in all at the old Town Hall and the girls we left
behind us.

In the room below with the chairs in a row sat the famous
Town Commission
To build new schools and swimming pools was their whole
life's ambition
And manys the time a member said 'If I swear out loud don't
mind me'
Sure I often felt like swearing too at the girls we left behind us.

Ah the sound was grand of Bannan's Band and the music so
entrancing
Enticed us there on the Market Square to sing and keep on
dancing
Ah all is gone but still live on fond memories to remind us
Of stately Balls in the old Town Hall and the girls we left
behind us.

*A saddler by trade, Joe McEvoy from O'Moore Place was the caretaker for many
years. He died in June 1945, three months after the Hall burned down.*

MEMORIES

Silent and lone and deserted I find thee,
The bright lights have faded, all merriment gone.
There's nothing left now save bare walls to remind me
How days have passed swiftly and years have rolled on.
Only in dreams, and with heart full of sadness
Those glorious nights can I clearly recall
The music, the dancing, the laughter, the gladness
That rang from the depths of Portlaoighise's Town Hall.

We boasted no lounges, no cocktails or ices
And Jitterbug fans were unknown to us then.
But we'd porter and whiskey with ham and with spices
And things quite unknown to the staid upper ten.
When tired of the dancing we strolled in the moonlight
While famed Richard Bannan played 'After the Ball'
And Love's sweetest story was told till the sunlight
Stole silently into Portlaoighise's Town Hall.

And there underneath sat the old Town Commission
Who times out of number were making new rules.
In the middle of winter their only ambition
Was planning and building us new swimming pools.
And often their voices were heard in vexation
The same as the lively debate in the Dáil.
They never knew peace till they went on vacation
Away, far away, from Portlaoighise's Town Hall.

So only in dreams as in deep meditation
We pass thro' its portals and do not forget
Those glorious nights we recall with elation
Ah even its name brings a throb of regret.
Regret for the days that are gone now forever
Of whist drive, of concert, of party, or ball
But long years of absence or time cannot sever
Our memories and dreams of Portlaoighise's Town Hall.

NOTES

1. *Leinster Express*. February 6, 1886.
2. *Ibid*.
3. Originally known as the Fisk Free Colored School for the education of freed slaves, the university still exists today. The school was named in honour of General Clinton B. Fisk who made premises available to the school, as well as establishing the first free schools for both white and black children in Tennessee.
4. *Leinster Express*. March 13, 1886.
5. In a letter to *The Irish Times*. January 23, 1912.
6. *Leinster Express*. February 2, 1901.
7. *Ibid*. January 6, 1912.
8. The Hall catered for other sports as well. In December, 1909, there was a big attendance at a meeting to establish an Association Football club in the town and, over the years, the local Table Tennis and Badminton club played matches there. If you preferred something more sedentary, the same club ran regular Whist Drives.
9. *Leinster Express*. November 11, 1906.
10. Often referred to as the first narrative feature film, and the first production to use specially-built sets.
11. *Leinster Express*. December 26, 1908.
12. *Nationalist and Leinster Times*. January 7, 1922.
13. *Leinster Express*. February 3, 1923.
14. *Ibid*. August 12, 1944.
15. They put on their shows in the Coliseum Ballroom instead.
16. Mrs. Elizabeth McCormack was renowned as musical director of countless productions in the town. Many people I've spoken to have vivid recollections of her seated regally at the piano, her cigarette drooping ash. The family headstone, incidentally, is adorned with musical notation.
17. Public swimming baths were first mooted at a meeting in the Town Hall in January, 1910, but it wasn't until July, 1971 that the municipal swimming pool was officially opened. It was replaced by the present Leisure Centre in December, 2007.
18. He was living on the Heath at that time, but my efforts to trace him or any family members have, so far, been unsuccessful.
19. Sung to the air of *The Girl I left Behind Me*. Originally an Irish tune that became popular as a marching song in the American Civil War.

ONE HUNDRED FACTS ABOUT PORTLAOISE

1. The town grew up around a fort established by English settlers in 1548. In 1557 it was named Maryborough in honour of Queen Mary.

2. After the rebellion of 1798, it was widely believed that juries in Maryborough were too eager to convict. Lawyers and other officials openly sported Orange emblems in court, and suspects were often sentenced to death simply to make examples of them.

3. If you needed a plumber back in 1955, the name was Bond, James Bond, 53, Clonminam.

4. My father grew up in Clonroosk House just off the Ballyfin Road. In the 1730's, it was 'fit for the residence of any gentleman of moderate fortune and family' and the home of Thomas Mosse, father of Bartholomew, who founded the Rotunda maternity hospital in Dublin.

5. April 8, 1915. A service is conducted in Maryborough Methodist Church by evangelist 'Gipsy' Smith. Born in a tent in Epping Forest, London, he was raised in a Romany camp and never spent as much as a single day in school.

6. January, 1921. Queen's County Coursing Club invites people to 'come in your thousands to Maryborough and see the best greyhounds in Ireland running for the Midland Cup'.

7. July, 1861. Twenty-year-old Albert Edward, Prince of Wales, marches with his regiment, the Grenadier Guards, from the Curragh Camp to military manouvres on The Heath. The troops also parade through Maryborough where, according to *The Irish Times*, 'every window was occupied by ladies and gentlemen from the surrounding country, while thousands of the peasantry thronged the streets and leading thoroughfares, breathless with anxiety to get a glimpse of the Prince'. Forty years later, on the death of his mother Queen Victoria, Albert Edward, known as 'Bertie', became the philandering Edward VII.

8. *An triú lá déag de Mí an Mheithimh, 1948. Feis Mór Laoise i bPortlaoise. Ceol, Rinncí, Teanga, Amhránaíocht, Bannaí, Stair agus Drámaí.*

9. May 2, 1763. A Freemasonry Lodge is established in the town. The Brethren meet in an upstairs room of the Bear Inn owned by Mr. George Frost. Today, the Lodge rooms are situated in Church Street.

10. December, 1949. The local James McIntosh Cumann of Fianna Fáil proposes to the Town Commission that Coote Street be renamed Lalor Street (or James Fintan Lalor Street, depending on which local newspaper you read).

11. While the Revolution rages in France, pupils in Mrs. Trousdell's Boarding school are learning English, Writing, Arithmetic, Geography, Drawing, Music and Dancing,

Tambour, Filigree, Embroidery and 'all kinds of fashionable work'. She also undertakes to look after the health and morals of her pupils.

12. Charles Corcoran, a late 19th century solicitor in the town, was the grandfather of actor Roddy McDowell.

13. July 8, 1782. The 'Gentlemen of the Queen's County' meet in Maryborough to 'consider the most proper and effectual mode of obtaining relief for the sufferers by the late dreadful fire in the town'.

14. January 27, 1903. After their dinner, two hundred inmates of Maryborough Gaol suffer 'violent vomiting and paralytic distortions'. It is discovered that spraying powder used on the prison farm had been repackaged as pepper.

15. December, 1945. Portlaoise Film Society publishes the first issue of its monthly journal, *Scannán*.

16. December, 1846. A man is found dead in Tea Lane. The subsequent newspaper report is the epitome of Victorian melodrama: 'there was neither fire nor candlelight in the wretched hovel; no drink to allay the death-thirst of his parched lips but cold water; while his bed was a wisp of straw on the damp floor...'

17. September, 2004. As part of its bicentenary celebrations, St. Peter's Church hosts a Flower Festival (visited by President Mary McAleese on September 27) and concerts by the Tullamore Gospel Choir.

18. 1850. Frederick Bourne's inn and coaching establishment at Boughlone is turned into an auxiliary workhouse. Many of

the inmates are buried in unmarked graves in the small graveyard there.

19. 1922. Rowe's Jewellers (opposite where Dunamaise Arts Centre is today) guarantee to develop photographs 'free from scratches and finger marks'.

20. January, 1886. The entire contents of the recently-closed Annebrook House on the Stradbally Road are put up for auction. This house (and another at Woodville) had constituted The Midland Retreat, a progressive asylum run by Dr. Jacob. Annebrook was for 'the reception of Ladies; Woodville for Gentlemen' and, 'neither house presents any of the usual characters of a Lunatic Asylum… restraint is not, under any circumstances, practised'.

21. October 1985. *Meitheal na Samhna*, the first Laois Arts Festival, is launched in the town. The festival's slogan was ISTHATYOUMOVIN? Can you remember why?

22. November 2, 1813. A 'numerous meeting' in the courthouse of the Roman Catholics of the Queen's County calls for 'the total and unqualified repeal of all the statutes which infringe, directly or indirectly, the sacred rights of religious freedom'. Secretary of the meeting is John Dunne.

23. Tea Lane is actually a misnomer. It was named because a smaller lane behind the houses in Grattan Street met it, forming the letter T.

24. 1895. Richard Fennell becomes the first Catholic postmaster in the town. According to the *Nationalist and Leinster Times*, this was achieved despite 'the bitter opposition and wire-pulling of the local Freemason Lodge'.

25. In the 1930's, the Yellow Lough was filled in to make way for the new County Hospital.

26. July 30, 1919. The twenty-third annual show of the Queen's County Agricultural Society is held in the Show Grounds near the railway station.

27. October, 1787. Tenders sought for the supply of 100,000 bricks for the construction of the new courthouse.

28. November, 1883. A meeting in Stradbally adopts a resolution to build a tramway between there and Maryborough.

29. August, 1914. Russell's Sawmills – beside the railway bridge in Grattan Street – are completely gutted by fire. Efforts to extinguish the inferno were futile 'as there was only one hose procurable'.

30. July, 1820. John Butterfield is hanged for stealing five pigs.

31. August, 1997. The new cobblelocked Main Street is completed at a cost of €1.6 million. The *Leinster Express* remarks on the wonderful carnival atmosphere at the official opening when hundreds thronged the street. But some could see beyond the pageantry, the lasers, the jazz and vintage cars. 'Those yokes won't last', I overheard one old townie, 'they'll be at it again in no time'.

32. December 5, 1962. Owned by future Taoiseach, Albert Reynolds (and boasting a 'Maple Floor, Continental Lighting and the Royal Showband'), Danceland opens on the New Road. It was demolished in 1970.

33. December 12, 1997. The County Council formally buries a time capsule under the footpath on Main Street (outside the Sally Gardens pub, facing into Church Street). The capsule contains, *inter alia*, newspaper articles, supermarket receipts, my wife's poetry, parking discs, golf balls, posters, price lists, badges and buttons, unconsecrated bread and a novel by yours truly. Fitzmaurice Place is officially opened on the same day.

34. August, 1914. John Redmond inspects 3,000 National Volunteers in the town. During his address, he announces that he has several thousand rifles in his possession for distribution.

35. January, 1953. Sixteen women became violently sick from gas poisoning in the Coliseum Cinema.

36. May 16, 1815. Bartholomew Bull of Maryborough marries Charlotte Grandy from Duncannon, County Wexford. It is the groom's fourth marriage; he is 75, his bride 18.

37. March, 1987. Judge Kevin O'Higgins rules that, 'on the balance of probabilities', the fire which gutted the Coliseum Cinema in December, 1985 was 'started maliciously'.

38. 1859. The Presentation Convent is lit by gas for the first time.

39. September, 1815. Captain Thomas Cassan dies from wounds received at the Battle of Waterloo. The Cassan family lived at Sheffield House, Capoley.

40. September 29, 1979. To honour the Pope's arrival in Ireland, all licensed premises in Laois remain closed from

10.30 a.m. to 3.30 p.m.

41. June, 1870. A meeting, 'largely attended by the young men of the town', decides to form Maryborough Cricket Club.

42. December, 1963. A County Councillor proclaims that the historic Infirmary building – opposite the prison on the Dublin Road – 'should have a bomb put under it'.

43. June, 1876. A travelling repairer of rosary beads is accused of murdering a nun inside the convent. During his trial, he maintains that God wanted nuns and he was on a mission to send them to Him.

44. November 2, 1956. Titania, 'World's Fattest Girl (36 st 8 lbs)' is on view from 3 to 12 pm. Adults sixpence. Children threepence.

45. March 7, 1927. In a letter to the Editor of the *Leinster Express*, County Librarian Helen Roe stresses the historical importance of local documents. She writes: 'Today will soon belong to the past and much that we today consign to the waste paper basket would be of tremendous interest to students in time to come'.

46. May, 1911. The Queen's County Sanatorium for Consumptives (in the grounds of the Infirmary) is formally opened by Lady Aberdeen.

47. November, 1912. The new sanatorium is completely destroyed by fire.

48. November, 1962. The town is shocked by the discovery of

a young woman's strangled body on The Heath.

49. October 17, 1873. An advertisement seeking a new compositor for the *Leinster Express* stipulates that 'none but sober men need apply'.

50. December 15, 2007. The new statue of James Fintan Lalor at County Hall is officially unveiled by Tánaiste and Minister for Finance, Brian Cowen.

51. August, 1844. A crowd of 4,000, assembled for a cockfight near the town, disperses after being addressed by Rev. Dunne, Parish Priest of Raheen.

52. July, 2009. Artist Mannix Flynn withdraws his show, *State Meant*, in protest after Dunamaise Arts Centre Director, Louise Donlon, insists that one particular piece be displayed on the first floor and not in the foyer.

53. May, 1886. Joseph Buckley's shop on Main Street advertises the latest styles in dolmans, stockinette jackets, paletots, aigrettes, feathers and bird's wings.

54. September, 2011. A body, estimated to be more than 2,000 years old, is discovered in Cúl na Móna bog.

55. February 2, 1863. A soiree is held in the Zion Chapel, Tower Hill, to celebrate its re-opening after extensive repairs.

56. June 14, 1861. The town is beset by a thunderstorm that lasts for seven hours. Such was its ferocity that, according to *The Irish Times*, 'the oldest inhabitant, even those who have seen foreign parts, could not recall its likes'.

57. January, 1965. Laois County Council adopts a proposal to build an underground public convenience in the Market Square 'with a three foot high surround' and a roof decorated with 'shrubs of the all-the-year-round variety.' It was 'with pleasure' that the *Leinster Express* reported that 'the news was definite' and the project would 'prove a landmark in local history'.

58. April 11, 1850. For the murder of her husband, Catherine Moore is 'launched into eternity' at Maryborough Gaol. A crowd of a thousand watches the execution.

59. April, 1988. The Portlaoise Dixieland Jazz Festival guarantees everyone 'a swinging time'.

60. 1847. The recently-opened Bank of Ireland office is situated in Quality Row (Grattan Street today). It subsequently moved to Coote Street and Bank Place before its current location on Main Street.

61. February, 2008. The former Malthouse/Minch Norton site at Coote Street is put on the market for €25m. The site is still vacant today (January, 2016).

62. June, 1859. Henry William Talbot, founder of the *Leinster Express* in 1831, dies in Kingstown. His remains are brought by train to Maryborough and interred in St. Peter's church-yard in the Market Square.

63. January, 1989. Monarch Properties announce plans to build a shopping centre in Railway Street (where Wesley Terrace and the Heritage Hotel Leisure Centre stand today). This, of course, never happened.

64. July, 1789. About a mile outside the town, two gentlemen are robbed by 'a gang of five footpads who took their cash and watches and obliged them to strip and left them almost naked in their carriage'.

65. October 19, 2000. According to *The Irish Times*, the benefits of living in Portlaoise for commuters include a very attractive town centre, good cultural and sporting facilities, cheaper houses, and the Dunamaise Arts Centre. All of which make the town 'a safe bet for anyone looking for a change of lifestyle'. Negatives are lack of parking, schools bursting at the seams, and the journey to and from Dublin that adds at least three hours to the working day.

66. 1825. Sir Walter Scott, author of such classic novels as *Rob Roy* and *Ivanhoe*, spends some time as the guest of Judge Moore at Lamberton Park, near Ratheniska. He is 'greatly delighted with the scenic beauties of this neighbourhood'.

67. June 1, 2014. Town Councils are abolished. This polarised local opinion, but was also responsible for a probable question in future table quizzes: name the three-times Mayor of Portlaoise (Chairman of Town Council) who was also the last man to hold that position?

68. 1913. At the opening of the Assizes in July, Mr. Justice Moloney is presented with a pair of white gloves. This old tradition symbolised the fact that there was no criminal business before the court. The judge said that he was happy that the county was in a state of peace, order and prosperity: 'There is no boycotting, no intimidation, no cattle-driving... nothing whatever to disturb the maintenance of law and order'.

69. May, 1935. The *Leinster Express* runs a competition for readers. The prizes are free airplane flights from a field in Bloomfield. One of the conditions is that all entrants must agree to free the paper's proprietor from 'all liability in the event of an accident'.

70. March, 1905. The premises of Maryborough Workmen's Club in Railway Street (behind Aird's Hotel) are gutted by fire. All the club's property, including a billiard and two bagatelle tables, is destroyed.

71. December 4, 1840. Over one hundred members of Maryborough Teetotal Society sit down to a Temperance Dinner. In its report, the *Freeman's Journal* comments on the good order, generous feeling and clean appearance of those present.

72. 1904. The Shaw family buys Edghill and Smith's drapery shop in Lower Main Street. They remained in business there until 2013.

73. 1965. The Men's Confraternity has a membership of more than 2,000. Considered an anachronism after the Second Vatican Council, the Confraternity was disbanded in the 1970's.

74. May, 1864. Dr. John Jacob writes to the *Freeman's Journal* complaining about vandalism in the town perpetrated by those who 'prefer nightly depredation to daily industry'.

75. June, 1962. Rev. Dr. Thomas Keogh, Bishop of Kildare and Leighlin, formally blesses the site and turns the first sod of the new Catholic church.

76. New Year's Day, 1772. A servant absconds with money belonging to Mr. Robert Graves who promptly publishes a description of the culprit: 'a low, squat fellow, about 20 years of age, wears his own hair which is black, and went off in a brown Cloth Coat, with a crimson faded Coler [*sic*], a double-breasted drab-colour Waistcoat and leather Breeches'.

77. December, 1933. The Ruddell Tobacco Company interviews local tobacco growers with a view to purchasing their crops.

78. 1834-1872. Founded by Patrick Quigley, and published sporadically between those years, the *Leinster Independent* was the Nationalist and Catholic nemesis of the staunchly Unionist *Leinster Express*. Patrick Quigley died at his home, Bloomfield House, in 1874.

79. December 14, 1965. Terry Wogan officially opens John Cole's 'Green Star' Superstore at 90-91, Main Street. It soon becomes the local centre of the Green Shield Stamps loyalty scheme.

80. July 2, 1861. Parish Priest Rev. Dr. Taylor lays the foundation stone of a new Parochial House in the area known as the Golden Croft. This fine white house – 'Maryville' – is situated behind the CBS and is clearly visible from Railway Street. It was built by local contractor, Edward Craven.

81. February 27, 1897. The first person to be buried in the new cemetery on the Stradbally road is a Christian Brother, Joseph Foley. The second is Patrick Doyle, a private in the 4th Leinster Regiment, who died in the Queen's County Infirmary on the Dublin Road.

82. 1936. The inhabitants of the insalubrious Lyster Lane are finally rehoused, many in the newly-built O'Moore Place.

83. July, 1779. The bogs between Maryborough and Mountmellick are poisoned to 'prevent Poachers from destroying the Game'.

84. November, 1914. Thirty-two merchants sign a document saying that they have 'unanimously decided to give no Xmas boxes owing to high prices and small profits, and the great necessity for economy'.

85. March, 1922. Serious disruption to train services due to a strike by coalmen at Maryborough and other stations.

86. April 12, 1804. For the manslaughter of a young fifer in the yeomanry corps of Stradbally, John Butler is sentenced to be 'burned in the hand and suffer one year's imprisonment'.

87. 1910. The most popular place for a swim in the town is the Green Mill pond, described by the Secretary of the County Council of the time as a 'a nasty pool'.

88. January 10, 1958. Douglas Hyde (1911-1996), not our first president, but a former leading member of the British Communist party now converted to Catholicism, gives a lecture in the Coliseum Cinema on the evils of the Red Menace.

89. February, 1920. John Styles saves a little boy from drowning in the swollen Triogue.

90. December, 1845. The infant son of a farmer living just outside the town is attacked and killed by the family pig. At

the inquest, the pig was presented as a deodand to Queen Victoria. In modern terms, the owner had to pay a fine – to the value of the animal – to the Crown. The practice was abolished in 1846.

91. Autumn, 1913. Plans are made to send hungry children to England for the duration of the Dublin Lockout. On October 25, Parish Priest, Monsignor Murphy, is informed that some children would be coming by motor car from Dublin to meet the Rosslare train in Maryborough. Word flies around the town and, within fifteen minutes, close on a thousand people assemble at the station to prevent such 'deportation'. No car appears; the next train is thoroughly searched but no sign of any children. Cheers are 'heartily given' for the Archbishop of Dublin and Monsignor Murphy, and the crowd marches away.

92. July 25, 1957. Duffy's Circus – in Shelly's field on the Green Road – presents a Rock 'n' Roll demonstration by Freddie and Sadie. Two years later, the featured attraction is the Giant Frog, the Creature from Outer Space.

93. December 26, 1859. Catholics hold a meeting in the town to 'express our sympathy with our Holy Father, the Pope, under his present sore trials and persecutions'. Which presumably refers to Pius IX's struggle to retain sovereignty over the Papal States. They eventually became part of the Kingdom of Italy.

94. March 7, 1905. Mr. Richard White gives a lecture, *With a Camera in Russia*, in the Lecture Hall, Church Street.

95. June, 1895. Local business people protest at 'the great wrong being inflicted on our town and county' by the transfer

of the staff of the 4th Battalion of the Leinster Regiment from Maryborough Barracks to Birr.

96. February, 1963. *Ben Hur* is showing in the Coliseum .

97. October, 1876. The District Sanitary Officer reports that the municipal sewerage system is so defective that 'the consequences might be disastrous if the town were visited with an epidemic'.

98. January 1, 1915. A recruiting poster promises 'a trip to Germany in the spring for a few sportsmen… rifles and ammunition supplied free… good shooting and hunting… all hotel expenses and railway fares paid… only a limited number (one million) required… all desirous of partaking report themselves to the Barracks, Maryborough'.

99. September, 1860. A telegraph station is established in the town. Messages can now be transmitted 'to any other station in the kingdom and, *vice versa*, from any other station to Maryborough'.

100. 1871. After winning the Waterloo Cup for the third time, greyhound Master McGrath becomes so famous that his owner is asked to bring him to meet the Royal Family at Windsor Castle. On July 8, en route to his trainer's home in Waterford, 'the greatest canine celebrity which ever ran in slips' stops off in Maryborough railway station where townspeople are invited to come and see him.

Thanks to everyone who helped in any way with my research, especially those who patiently endured my endless questions. Any mistakes are all mine.

To see pictures of many of the places mentioned in this book please go to www.portlaoisepictures.com

ISBN-13: 978-1-5262-0210-9